SUGAR CREEK GANG
THE
BATTLE OF THE BEES

SUGAR CREEK GANG

THE
BATTLE OF THE BEES

Paul Hutchens

MOODY PRESS • CHICAGO

Original Title:
Sleeping Beauty at Sugar Creek

ISBN 0-8024-4830-5

15 16 17 Printing/LC/Year 89 88

Printed in the United States of America

1

It had been quite a while since I had been caught up in the whirlwind of a stormy Sugar Creek adventure, and it began to look like I might have to live through the rest of the summer without anything worrisome happening to me. As 'most any boy knows, one of the worst things that can happen to a boy is to have *nothing* happen to him.

Also, as 'most any boy knows, there are two kinds of adventures a boy can have around Sugar Creek. One is the hair-raising kind, that whams into him like a whirlwind surprises a pile of autumn leaves, picks him up, and tosses him into the middle of a problem or a mystery or a menace. It stirs up the boy to use his mind and muscles to help himself or somebody else out of whatever trouble he or somebody else is in.

The other kind of adventure is what my bushy-eyebrowed, reddish-brown-moustached, farmer father calls the "educational" type. "It's the *best* kind," he has told me maybe seventy-three times, "and it will do a boy a lot more good in the long run." My grayish-brown-haired mother calls it an "adventure of the mind."

But what boy wants a lot of *good* done to him! I'll have to admit that I would rather have the hair-raising, spine-tingling kind of adventure such as the gang has had quite a few of in the past several years. Maybe you've already heard about how we killed the fierce old, mad old mother bear and the sheep-stealing wildcat; how we licked the afternoon daylights out of a tough, town gang in the Battle of Bumblebee Hill; also all the nervous excitement we had when we tried to act out a poem every boy knows, and took a wet, pet lamb to school one day. We certainly found out it was against the rule, and it more than certainly didn't make everybody laugh and play—especially not the teacher. We even rode the world's longest chair lift at Aspen, Colorado, and helped solve the Wild Horse Canyon mystery.

And so, it began to look as if the rest of our summer vacation from school would be a very ordinary one, full of such ordinary things as mowing our own lawns for nothing, working in

6

our own gardens for nothing, and washing and drying dishes for nothing. One of my worst chores was to baby-sit with my baby sister for nothing; she was three years old and couldn't be baby-sat with anyway, because she never sat still long enough for anybody to sit *with* her.

I should explain that when my parents talked about educational adventures, they didn't mean reading and writing and arithmetic.

"All of life is a schoolroom," my father explained to me. "You can have an adventure in your *mind* every day, even while you are drying dishes or hoeing potatoes or plowing the black-seeded Simpson lettuce in the garden. Even while you're—"

Dad hesitated a few seconds, and while his sentence was still in midair, I cut in to suggest, "Or while I'm sitting on a log down at the mouth of the branch, with my line out in the water waiting for a bass to strike?"

My father's eyebrows dropped at my half joke; then he said something *very* educational, and which, before you get through reading this story, you will decide was maybe one of the most important things in the world for a boy or even a girl to know.

"Son," my dad's deep voice growled out to

me, "everything good or bad a boy ever does, starts in his mind, not in his muscles."

"Not even in his powerful biceps?" I asked, trying hard to say something humorous.

Because we were standing halfway between the iron pitcher pump and the grape arbor with its empty two-by-four crossbeam, six feet high, challenging me to leap up and skin a cat on it, I felt my biceps ordering me to give them a little exercise. Quick as anything, I whirled, leaped for the crossbeam, caught it, and in a jiffy had chinned myself three times. Then quick as scat I skinned the cat, swung my legs up and over, and in less time than it takes to write these few words, I was up and sitting and grinning down at Dad, feeling wonderful that my powerful biceps and my other muscles had done exactly what they had wanted to do. *"This* adventure started in my muscles," I said down to him.

Dad lowered his eyebrows up at me and said, "Wrong! Your muscles didn't do that. *You* did. Your mind wanted you to do it; and you, yourself—the you that is on the *inside* of you—ordered your muscles to do it, and they obeyed you."

Trying to be funny, I answered "I'm glad you admit I *have* a mind." I looked out across the treetops of our orchard toward the west

8

where Poetry, my almost best friend, lived; flexed my biceps; and felt one of the most wonderful feelings a boy ever feels, as I filled my lungs with clean, seven-o'clock-in-the-morning fresh air. Then, like our old red rooster does, I flapped my arms, lifted my face toward the sky, and let out a squawking, high-pitched cock-a-doodle-doo.

"That," I said to Dad, with a grin in my natural voice, "was an adventure of the *voice.*"

He shrugged and made it easy for me to come down by ordering me to. "There's something I want to show you before breakfast," he said, and led the way from where we were to the row of flaming hollyhocks that grew along the orchard fence just west of the grape arbor, which was about thirty-seven feet from the west side of our house. There we stopped—both of us sort of listening in the direction of the kitchen door to hear a woman's voice calling to us that breakfast was ready.

"Look," Dad began. He lifted a hollyhock leaf very carefully, like he does Charlotte Ann's cute little chin when he wants to see into her mischievous blue eyes. Charlotte Ann is my very cute baby sister I've already mentioned—my "first and worst," as Poetry describes her.

9

I focused my eyes on the large, coarse, round hollyhock leaf resting on Dad's forefinger. I was also looking at several large, circular, wide-open maroon flowers of which there were maybe thirteen on the tall hollyhock stalk.

"What am I supposed to see?" I said to Dad, yawning.

He answered, "Dew! Fresh, clean, dewdrops. See how damp this leaf is?"

When I answered, "What *of* it?" I was surprised at what he said next.

"Notice this leaf is as wet on the *inferior* side as on the *superior.*" He probably thought I was old enough to learn the meaning of those two rather long words.

Then Dad went leaping and diving into the educational adventure he wanted me to enjoy with him, kind of like a boy already out in the middle of Sugar Creek calling back to another boy, "Come on in, the water's fine!"

"The hollyhock," Dad's deep voice rumbled, "is a Chinese herb, a garden plant of the mallow family. In Egypt its leaves are used for food—after they're cooked, of course. The hollyhock's botanical name is the *Althea rosea,* and like most flowers, it is symbolic."

Most of Dad's words were too long for me

to understand, and it seemed like it wasn't going to be a very interesting adventure of the mind. It didn't have enough action in it—nothing to use my muscles on. I yawned and started to say so to Dad, but yawned again instead, and squinted at the hollyhock leaf, which I was surprised to notice did have as much dew on the under side as it did on its top side.

"Furthermore," Dad went on, "the symbolism of the hollyhock is *ambition*—and that's the first half of today's educational adventure."

I had my eye on the tall hollyhock stalk right next to the one Dad was using as his object lesson. *"What's* the first half of my adventure?" I asked. My mind was in the kitchen where frying country sausage was sending its fragrance all the way out to our outdoor schoolroom.

"Ambition," Dad answered with a teacher-like voice. "Every time you see a hollyhock anywhere, you're supposed to say to yourself, 'Bill Collins, don't be a lazy good-for-nothing! Be ambitious! Wake up your mind and put it to work to be somebody worthwhile in life. Don't be a drone lying around a hive!' Does that make sense to you?"

"Does *what* make sense?" I asked in

answer, but I thought I knew what he meant. He expected me to be a hollyhock kind of boy—not an idler or a worthless, shiftless, lazy good-for-nothing, like he had just said.

Well, Dad and Mom and I were pretty good friends. We would sometimes have a joke between us for a whole day. All three of us laughed to each other at different things that happened around the place, or at things one or the other had read or heard somewhere. So, even though I was sort of sleepy and also hungry, I looked up at the grin under Dad's moustache and asked, "Are you sure you're interested in my being an ambitious boy, or are you thinking about the garden out there, hoping somebody's only son will show a little more interest in it?"

"The garden, of course," was Dad's good-natured answer. Then he added, "Ambition in a boy's mind can do a better job controlling his muscles than three beech switches hanging on the gun rack in the toolshed."

My mind's eye looked right through the ponderosa pine wall of the toolshed and saw Dad's gun rack with two shotguns and my .22 rifle on it. Lying across the lower horns of the rack, I saw three innocent-looking beech switches, and remembered how Dad had once remarked to Poetry's father, "The guns are for wild animals, and the switches are for wild boys."

Right then Mom called from the kitchen door that breakfast was ready. It probably would be pancakes and sausage, milk, and maybe some kind of fresh fruit, such as yesterday's just-picked cherries, which I'd picked myself from the cherry tree that grew not more than twenty feet from the hollyhock's last, tall, spire-like stalk.

"One minute," Dad called to Mom. "I have to assign tomorrow's lesson!"

Dad then quickly assigned it to me, seeming to be in more of a hurry than before Mom had called. I took my small notebook out of my shirt pocket and wrote down what he had told me.

On the way back to the boardwalk that led to our kitchen's back door, I was remembering Dad's assignment which was, "Look up page 204 in *The Green Treasury* in our upstairs library and study it. Also look up the word *dew* in our unabridged Webster; then read William Cullen Bryant's poem, 'To a Waterfowl.' "

Tomorrow I was to tell my teacher-father what, if any, new ideas had come to me.

Before going into the house to pancakes,

sausage, fruit, and whatever else Mom would have ready, Dad and I stopped for a fast minute at the low, round-topped table near the iron pitcher pump where there was a washbasin, a bar of soap, and a towel. There I washed my already-clean face and hands. That was one of the rules at our house; a certain red-haired, freckle-faced boy I knew got to wash his face and hands before he was allowed to sit at the table three times a day, seven days a week, three hundred sixty-five days a year. Say, did you ever figure up how many times you've had to do that since you were old enough to be told? Even in one year, it'd be over a thousand times!

"You first," I said to my father, since he was the oldest and was more used to cold water than I was.

While Dad was washing his hands and face, I stopped to study the leaves of Mom's row of salvia growing at the other end of her horseradish bed. When I lifted the chin of one of the green leaves, what to my wondering eyes should appear on the underside of the leaf but as much dew as there was on top!

Later, while I was sitting at the table with Dad and Mom—Charlotte Ann was still asleep in her baby bed in the front bedroom—I said to Dad, "I'm already ready for tomorrow's lesson.

William Cullen Bryant was wrong when he wrote 'Whither, midst falling dew . . .' "

I knew that those four words are the first line of Bryant's "To a Waterfowl." I'd memorized it in school when I was little.

"Dew," I said to Dad around a bit of pancake, "doesn't do what he said it did."

Mom, not knowing what on earth—or under a hollyhock or salvia leaf—Dad and I were talking about, looked at me across the table and asked, "What kind of talk is that, 'Do doesn't do what he said it did?"

Our senses of humor came to life, and for a few seconds Dad and I had a good laugh at Mom's expense. Dad asked her, "How do you spell *do,* my dear? Do you spell dew *do* or do you spell do *dew?"*

Mom's face was a blank, except for the question marks and exclamation points on it. Her kind of pretty eyebrows went down and a nervous little crinkle was running up and down her forehead.

Dad explained what he and I meant, but for some reason, her sense of humor didn't come to life; so we changed the subject and went on eating our sausage and pancakes and cherries.

Because I was a boy with a boy's mind with more important things on it than dew which didn't fall at all but condensed instead, I felt the outdoors calling me to come and enjoy it.

There was, for instance, a little brown path made by boys' bare feet, that ran as straight as a crooked cow path through the woods to the spring. It began on the other side of the rail fence on the other side of the road and twisted and dodged along, round and round, till it came to a hill that led down to the Black Widow Stump and on to the leaning linden tree.

Beginning at the linden tree, another path scooted east along a high rail fence to a wild crab apple tree and on to the place where the gang squeezed through the fence to get to the bayou.

Still another path ran from the leaning linden tree down a steep incline to the spring, and from the spring, after you eased through a barbed wire fence, a cool path ran between the bayou and the creek through tall marsh grass and all kinds of weeds to a clearing that bordered Dragonfly's father's cornfield. It ended at a well-worn grassy place under the Snatzerpazooka tree, where we had some of our most important meetings, and where we left our clothes when we went in swimming.

That very place was the place where, at two o'clock that afternoon, the gang was supposed to meet—all of us that could—and dicuss plans to spend tomorrow night at Old Man Paddler's cabin far up in the hills beyond the cave and the sycamore tree, and on the other side of the swamp.

All the whole wonderful Sugar Creek playground was sort of in my mind while I was at the breakfast table that morning — the morning of the beginning of the story of the Battle of the Bees.

In a sad corner of my mind, though, was something else—a garden begging a boy my size (with or without ambition) to come and do something about the small weeds, which, since the last rain, were growing twice as fast as the black-seeded Simpson lettuce, the Ebenezer onions, and the Golden Bantam sweet corn.

In the educational section of my mind, was a row of hollyhock with maybe a hundred many-colored flowers in full bloom, all the flowers seeming to have voices calling me to get out into the garden as soon as I could. "Ambition, Bill Collins! Ambition! Don't be an idle good-for-nothing! Don't be a drone lazying around at the door of a beehive!"

I'd seen hundreds of dopey drones lying around the beehives in Dad's apiary. While the worker bees were as busy as bees flying in and out, gathering honey, and helping pollinate the clover in Harm Groenwold's field on the other side of the lane, those lazy, good-for-nothing drones did nothing at all.

Sitting at the breakfast table that morning, I didn't have the slightest idea that bees and hives, Charlotte Ann, and a home run I was going to knock that afternoon were going to give me an exciting adventure of mind and muscle such as I'd never had before in all my half long life.

2

You would hardly imagine that an ordinary breakfast at our house would be so important to a boy—the ordinary things we said and thought—but they were. You can see *how* important and how they got mixed up in this story, if you will imagine yourself to be a ghost somewhere up in the air above our table, watching and listening. Keep your ghost eyes and ears open now, so you won't miss anything.

First, you see Mom in her chair between the range and the table where we are having breakfast. She is stirring her coffee; Dad is wiping his reddish-brown moustache with his napkin; and across the table the long way from him, is a red-haired, freckle-faced boy named Bill. The boy's plate is empty, and his silverware lying across it like you are supposed to place it when you have good manners.

Between Mom and Dad, if you want to, you

can see my sister Charlotte Ann's empty high chair. Lying on the chair's large wooden tray is a very old, gray, clothbound book open near the middle.

Out of that book for several weeks now, our family had been taking turns reading, getting thoughts and ideas for what we call "garden time," which some families call "family devotions."

"It's the time we cultivate our heart's gardens," was Mom's way of explaining it.

Sometimes our garden times were interrupted by Charlotte Ann waking up, or being already awake and at the table with us and not behaving herself; sometimes our thoughts would explode like a punctured soap bubble by the phone ringing two long longs and a very short short, and it would be some Sugar Creek Gang mother wanting to talk or listen to my mother about different things mothers like to talk about and listen to; sometimes we were interrupted by a noise out at the barn, such as Old Red Addie and her pigs squealing for their breakfast.

Once in a while there might be a boy out at our front gate near the walnut tree, or he might get all the way to our iron pitcher pump and be pumping away, getting himself a drink before I'd see or hear him.

Our garden time never lasted very long, just long enough for us to find a live seed to plant or a weed to pull out, which was Mom's way of saying it. Also, we were supposed to get a new thought of some kind and think about it every now and then during the day. "Clean thoughts," Dad had said quite a few times, "help keep a boy's mind clean."

Well, as soon as garden time at our breakfast table was over that morning—as you would have known if you'd been a ghost there and watching—you'd have seen three people with their heads bowed and their eyes closed and heard one of us making a short prayer; then you'd have heard me excuse myself and seen me go outdoors to the toolshed to get the one-shoveled, one-wheeled hand cultivator, to push it out into our actual garden and go to work.

While I was still in the toolshed, I stood for a few seconds looking at Dad's two shotguns on the gun rack, also at my .22, and just below it, the three beech switches he hardly ever used anymore. They might just as well be broken into pieces and burned.

It seemed for a second or six that my .22 was talking to me, saying, "You'd better take me with you Friday night. Remember the fierce old, mad old mother bear the gang stumbled onto a few summers ago? If Big Jim hadn't had his gun along, Little Jim might have been killed. Remember the fierce-fanged wildcat you killed? Who knows what you might need me for up in the hills away from everybody in the middle of the night?"

In my mind also, I could sort of hear the three beech switches talking, too, and saying, "Ambition, Bill Collins!" It was the same thing the hollyhocks out along the fence were supposed to be saying.

In a little while I was all the way out to the garden, pushing the plow back and forth between the rows of black-seeded Simpson lettuce, the Ebenezer onions, and the Golden Bantam sweet corn. In my mind as I worked, my .22 was still talking and warning me of some danger we might run into Friday night.

But danger was something I wouldn't dare mention to my parents—especially not to my mother. You see, she would worry about me, since mothers are made that way and can't help it.

In my mind also, were two words we had found in the gray book that morning. Mom had liked those two words so well she'd said them over and over again. She even said them several times sort of half to herself, while she was standing at the stove with her back to us pouring herself another cup of coffee. Those two words, if you didn't happen to hear them, were *slumbering splendor.*

The sentence the words were in and which Dad had read to us, went something like this, "There may be any amount of slumbering splendor in us, but it cannot get out because of sin."

"It's just like a lily bulb," Mom had thought of to say, and her spoon stirring the sugar and cream in her cup squeaked a little as she talked. "Inside the dry-looking, sometimes ugly bulb, there is a beautiful lily, snow-white and fragrant. But as long as it's asleep in the bulb, wrapped round and round with layer after layer of its self life, it cannot get out." She had a faraway look in her eyes as she said it, like she was seeing something wonderful for the first time.

I could tell that Mom and Dad were getting more out of what they were talking about than I was, but it *did* seem pretty wonderful that a dried-up old lily bulb or a tulip bulb could grow out of themselves and become something different.

"In other words," Dad looked at me to say, "when you look at anything, you're supposed to see more than you see. When your two gray-green eyes see a tulip bulb lying in a box with a dozen others, your inner eye sees the future—a border of tulips somewhere, with a dozen two-foot-tall tulip stalks, each one holding up a blue or yellow or red or white or purple cup, all the cups empty and trying to catch as much rain and sunshine as they can hold."

Mom cut in then to say, "Isn't that pretty flowery language?"

Dad's friendly answer was, "We're talking about pretty flowers, aren't we?"

Right then, our garden time was stopped by a familiar sound coming from the front bedroom—like a cat sounds when you accidentally step on its tail; also like "six little pigs in the straw with their mother with bright eyes, curly tails tumbling on each other" and squealing for their breakfast. It was Charlotte Ann coming out of the night into the day.

*　　*　　*

Back and forth, forth and back, push, grunt, walk, push, grunt, sweat—my one-shoveled plow crawled back and forth across the garden, while all the time I was straining my inner eye to see if I could see more than I saw.

If there were a lot of sleeping splendor in every boy, it was also maybe in everything a boy looked at. Also, the boy might even try to wake up a little of it.

Right then, I spied our old black-and-white cat sleeping in the sun on the sloping cellar door, seventeen feet from the iron pitcher pump. I stooped, picked up a clod of dirt, and slung it across the yard, where it landed with a noisy thud less than twelve inches from Mixy's early morning nap.

Talk about sleeping splendor waking up! Mixy came to the fastest cat life a cat ever came to, leaped into the air, and took off like a streak toward Mom's flowerpot table beside the toolshed.

Right that second I heard a fluttering of wings, and a robin with an orange breast landed with a *kerplop* not more than fifteen feet from me behind me, and started helping herself to a wriggling fishworm my plow had just unearthed.

My plow had wakened a sleeping fishworm, and when I saw it, I saw more than I saw. In a few fast flashes of my inner eye, I saw it wriggling on a boy's hook far out and down in the water in the fishing hole near the mouth of the branch of the creek. I saw a monster sunfish make a dive for it and even saw seven fish on a stringer.

But the mother robin, seeing the worm, had seen five baby robins in the nest in the plum tree with five hungry mouths wide open and cheeping for food.

It was sort of like a game I was playing, and a little later I came to, to find out I had plowed my way back and forth across the garden thirteen or fourteen times without knowing it. And it hadn't even seemed like work.

I hadn't even heard Dad coming—didn't know he was there until suddenly I saw him standing like a fence post at the end of the garden gate, watching me.

"Good work, son!" he called to me, and his gruff voice was like music. There is probably nothing a boy would like to hear more than one of his parents praising him for something.

"My sleeping splendor," I called jokingly from where I was stooped over pulling a small smartweed from an Ebenezer onion, "has just come to life!"

Then with Dad's compliment pushing me like a breeze blowing a cloud of dust, I grabbed the plow handles and went swooshing down the row to the other end. My shovel was turning up fishworms, the larvae of June beetles, and a lot of other underground insect life that lived in our garden.

Dad waited till I came panting back before he said anything else; then in a very fatherly voice he announced, "Your mother and I have to run in to town right after lunch. I need another quart of paint for the toolshed, and we have to have a screen for the front bedroom window. It's just too hot these summer days with the window shut, and the flies and mosquitoes get in when it's open. And your mother wants to get the groceries while the bargains are on. You know how Charlotte Ann is in the supermarket, so we're leaving her here with you. You won't mind baby-sitting with her?"

His tone of voice had a question mark on the end of his sentence, but I knew it was an order. I, Bill Collins, who had planned to meet with the gang at two o'clock to go in swimming and to help make plans for Friday night's all-night sleep in Old Man Paddler's cabin, was going to have to baby-sit with a baby that couldn't be baby-sat with!

Suddenly something inside of me woke up —and it wasn't anything that could be spelled

27

with the letters *s-p-l-e-n-d-o-r*! Out of my mouth like a baseball off a fast bat, there flew a sizzling exclamation, *"Baby-sit!* That's not fair, when the gang is meeting at the Snatzer-pazooka tree at two o'clock!"

It was the stormiest temper explosion I'd had in a long time, and it had happened just when I'd been feeling better inside than for a long time.

Now any boy knows that a sentence full of hot words coming out of his mouth at his father, is like poking a stick into a bumblebees' nest—the bumblebees' nest being the boy's father. And that boy is likely to get stung several fast, sharp times with a beech switch or something.

There isn't a boy in the whole Sugar Creek territory that would know that any better than Theodore Collins' son. My temper picked me up and tossed me around in the air like I was a last year's leaf in a whirlwind.

My hands on the plow handles were gripping it so tight, that when I looked down at them the knuckles were white; my teeth were set, and my jaw muscles were in a knot.

And then something very strange happened — something I decided afterward was maybe one of the most wonderful things that can happen to a boy. As fast as lightning there flashed into my mind one of the Ten Commandments we had studied in Sunday school the Sunday before. *"Honor thy father and thy mother!"* were the words that came to me, burning my temper into nothing.

I felt as weak as a sick cat and ashamed of myself. And what did my wondering ears hear but my own voice saying to Dad, "There's a lot of sleeping splendor in a baby sister. Tell Mom I'll be glad to stay with her, but I'll have to call the gang and explain why I can't come to the meeting."

Dad stared at me, his mouth open to say something else, but not even one word came out. Instead there were actual honest-to-goodness tears in his eyes, and I saw him swallow, like there was a lump in his throat.

For maybe a full thirty seconds, we just stared at each other. Then he spoke in a husky voice, saying, "God bless you, son. God bless you!"

He turned slowly, stooped, picked up a clod of dirt and broke it apart, and do you know what? There was a middle-sized fishworm in it. Before you could have said Jack Robinson, he stooped again, picked up an empty tin can lying at the gate, sifted a handful of dirt into it, dropped the worm in on top of the dirt and said, "You might watch while you're working. Save all the worms your plow or hoe turns up. You'll probably want to go fishing again before long."

I watched my father's broad back as he strode toward the house. I could hardly see him because of the mist in my eyes, and it seemed that in all my life before I had never liked my big-voiced, hard-muscled, callous-handed father as much as I did right that second—and I was feeling as clean inside as a cottontail dashing through the snow in our south pasture.

At the iron pitcher pump, Dad stopped, gave the handle a few fast squeaking strokes, took a drink, and tossed what water was left in the cup over the top of the water tank and into a puddle. In a second about fifteen white and sulphur butterflies fluttered in every direction of up there is—it's one of the happiest sights a boy ever sees around our farm.

I said something to myself then, not knowing I was going to say it, and it was, *Sleeping splendor! It's everywhere if you look for it, even in a father.*

I was whistling "Yankee Doodle" and slicing away at the sandy loam of the garden, when, from as far away as I was, I heard the phone ring in the house, and it was our number:

two long longs and a very short short. A jiffy later Mom's voice came quavering out to the garden where I was, calling, "Bill! Telephone!"

And away I went lickety-sizzle for the house, wondering who would be calling me and why. My feet were wings, and my heart was like a feather in the wind as I ran.

3

One of the happiest feelings I ever get is when the party line phone rings our number and it's for me. Just as I said, my feet are wings and my heart is a feather in the wind, as I drop whatever I'm doing and fly for our back door.

A galloping boy at our place stirs up quite a lot of excitement. About thirty-seven old hens and two roosters were gobbling up grains, greens, grubs, and grit in our barnyard, part of which is between the garden and the iron pitcher pump. When they saw and heard me coming, they parted before my flying bare feet like the waves of the Red Sea before the Children of Israel in the book of Exodus in the Bible; there was a squawking and cackling of scared chickens, as they stormed out of that part of the barnyard like they were trying to get out of the way of a runaway horse.

Mixy, who had gone back for her midmorning nap on the sloping cellar door, came to one of her nine lives; and like a black-and-white streak of four-footed fur, scooted for her hiding place under Mom's flowerpot table beside the toolshed; the butterflies near the pump were up and off again, and a second later our back screen door slammed behind me. In three leaps I was through the kitchen and into the living room, just in time for Mom, who herself was at the phone, to wave her arm at me and shush me.

Stunned, I stopped stock-still and stared, wondering *What on earth!*

"Yes," Mom was saying into the phone speaker, "I think that would be fine . . . No, I'm sure she didn't mean that—she just said that *if* I wanted to, I could bring a covered dish instead of a salad . . . No, I'd . . . that's all right, I'd rather cooperate. . . . Oh, Bill won't care. He likes any kind of pie — and besides . . . Oh yes, well, Stella Foote—you know how nice she always is about things like that . . . She *what?*"

Words were flying thick and fast between Mom and whatever other woman was on the other end of the line. It was the kind of women's talk that went on every day in our neighborhood. And as Dad had said to me one time,

"Women need to talk to women as much as boys need to play with boys."

I was standing beside the organ with the hymnbook on the rack open to "Let the Lower Lights Be Burning," and clearing my throat to ask Mom who wanted to talk to *me,* if anybody still did, when she came to long enough to notice I was still there. She quick covered the phone speaker with her free hand and whispered in my direction, "It's Mrs. Thompson. I asked to talk with her while you were coming. We'll be through in a minute" (one minute being the same as five at a time like that).

My mind's eye was seeing more than I saw. I saw all the way over to Poetry's house, and saw my barrel-shaped friend standing in *their* living room waiting for *his* mother to stop listening to *my* mother, while I was standing waiting for *my* mother to stop listening to *his.*

Pretty soon Mom made herself quit and handed me the phone.

"Good old Poetry!" I thought to myself, as I heard his duck-like voice coming over the wire to say, "Don't forget the meeting at you know where at you know when," he began.

"I can't come," I told him. "I have some work to do here, and my folks are going to be gone."

"Work!" he squawked. "Oh *no!* Not *work!*"

"Baby-sit!" I heard myself say in a disgruntled voice.

Then I explained that I was going to get to work in the garden and keep my eyes and ears awake while Charlotte Ann slept. "You just tell the gang I had to work," I ordered him. "You don't have to mention baby-sitting. They might not understand!" (You see, for some reason, one of the hardest things a boy ever can do is look after a little brother or sister when his folks are away and he'd rather be with his gang.)

Well, that was that, a rather sad that at that. I went back to the Ebenezer onions.

Trotting along beside and behind me, chattering and fussing a little and carrying a small pail and shovel was my shadow, as I called her. She was supposed to play in the sandpile in a big seven-by-seven box beside the garden gate while I worked.

Once, while I was on my knees pulling out two or three baby-sized jimsonweeds that were trying to smother out a stalk of Golden Bantam, I looked back across the tops of the husky, rustling corn blades at a tousled brownish head of hair in the sandbox; and for some reason, it was one of the prettiest sights

I ever saw. Maybe what I was feeling was what 'most any brother feels when he all of a sudden—without planning to at all—gets a big brother feeling of pride and actually likes his small-fry sister very much. It's a good feeling and good for a boy to have. All of a sudden, it also seemed like if anybody ever tried to hurt her or be mean to her or even scold her, my voice, my biceps, and my hard knuckled fists would go flying to her rescue.

She certainly was pretty, for a girl, I thought. Then I forgot I'd thought it when I saw the gate open and two chubby legs carry a brown-haired girl across the garden, the girl herself carrying a sand pail and shovel, walking toward me—not between the rows of garden stuff, but *on* the onions and lettuce and on anything that happened to be growing where her feet were going.

Like an explosion, I was up and running in her direction. I scooped her up and carried her squirming, wriggling thirty-two pounds back to the gate and out, and ordered, *"You* stay in your box, or else!"

Well, it looked like I wasn't going to have to wait till afternoon to start my baby-sitting job. I had already started it.

"Here, shadow," I said to her. "See how

much fun it is to fill your pail and dump it out over there in the corner?"

But she couldn't see what I saw, and there wasn't any hidden splendor in a sandbox, when she'd rather be out in the garden stepping on corn and lettuce and onions and on the potatoes that were just coming up.

I sat for a few minutes on the edge of her box, my bare feet in the sand, and as long as I did that, she seemed satisfied—except that she wanted to scoop sand on my feet, which I let her do, until all the toes were covered and the sand was halfway up to my knees.

Whenever I tried to leave her, she would start to fuss, so I sighed at her and said, "Listen, shadow, if you would just give me a chance, I could get my work done! How can you expect me to—"

That was as far as I got right then, because her shovel scooped up a brown centipede that started on a wriggling, twisting, fast-as-lightning scramble toward her.

Then is when she proved she was a girl, and I had a chance to prove I wasn't. It took only about seven seconds for my right arm to give that centipede a new home, which was somewhere out in the middle of the Simpson lettuce bed.

37

Maybe, I thought, *if I can scare her again, she'll decide to go into the house and I can get back to something else I don't want to do.* I looked around for a worm or a bug or something wiggly and spied on the dead, brown stem of a last year's purple vervain, a woolly bear caterpillar. Carefully, I broke off the stalk and carefully held it toward my sister; but do you know what? *That* didn't frighten her at all. Instead, she said, "'*Pillar* song! Sing the 'pillar song!"

The "'pillar song," as she calls it, is a cute little chorus Mom sings to her when she gives her a bath, to keep her mind off soap and water, which she doesn't like any better than a certain boy I know.

Just in case you would like to read the words of the "'pillar song," here they are:

> Said the striped caterpillar to the black-and-
> yellow bee,
> "Our colors are almost the same, and yet I do
> not see,
> Since both our coats are made of fuzz, you
> are the only one to buzz;
> To *bzzzz*—to *bzzzz*—to *bzzzzzzzzzzzz.*"

The second verse goes like this:

> To the striped caterpillar said the black-and-
> yellow bee,

"Indeed our colors are the same; you look a
    lot like me;
If you'll grow wings as well as fuzz, so you
    can fly, why, then you'll buzz;
You'll *bzzzzz*—you'll *bzzzz*—you'll
    bzzzzzzzzzzz!"

I made a long, low guttural buzzing sound
every time I came to the *z*'s, and that made that
little rascal of a sister very happy; her blue eyes
would light up, and she would giggle and act
like I was maybe the most wonderful person in
the world, until I wouldn't sing anymore, then I
wasn't.

While I was baby-sitting and standing and
talking and entertaining and not getting anywhere with Charlotte Ann, I was also trying to
remember what our family had learned at
garden time at the breakfast table.

Beside the sandbox, I saw growing a small
pink flower I knew was called the wood sorrel. I
pulled a half dozen of its cloverlike leaves and
began to chew them, which different members
of the gang were always doing, the leaves
having a sour juice in them which we liked.

"Here," I said to Charlotte Ann, holding
out to her one of the long, slender stalks I had
just broken off at the plant's roots, also one of
the long, slender stems on which was one lone

cloverlike leaf. "This wood sorrel is what the dictionary calls "the sleeping beauty," I explained to her in a teacher-like voice. "When you handle its leaves roughly, it closes up and looks like a wilted flower. That," I went on to Charlotte Ann who wasn't listening, "is why it's named that. It is very pretty, and it goes to sleep when a boy touches it. And that, my very pretty lady, is what I expect you to do this afternoon while Mom and Dad are in town shopping. If you *don't* go to sleep, I'll maybe have to handle you roughly so you will."

I stopped trying to teach her, when she scooped up a shovelful of sand, tossed it up in the air, and it came down all over everything, including my bare red head.

Because she was at the age when girls like to learn rough boys' games, I decided to try playing catch with her, using her soft rubber ball, and *that* made her happy. Every time she missed a catch, she would chase off after the ball like a trained puppy after a tossed ball or stick.

Dad came out of the house about that time, went into the toolshed, and came out with his bee-handling outfit. In only a few jiffies he had his smoker going, his bee gloves and bee veil on, a hive tool in one hand and one of Mom's large dishpans in the other. I knew he was going out

40

into the apiary to get some honey to take to town to sell.

Pretty soon he was all the way out to the bee garden where he had six hives, and was working around one of the hives, helping himself to the bees' hard-worked-for honey. "The bees are pretty hot-tempered this morning!" he called to where I was, a safe distance away. "There's a bee war on! You and your shadow better keep away today!"

"Don't worry!" I called back to him. He *needn't* have worried, either, on account of the last time there was a war on with one swarm of bees trying to steal another hive's honey, I'd gotten too close and had been stung five times. For a while I was so sick I almost fainted — being what is called allergic to beestings, which quite a few people in the world are. To me, a mad bee was about as scary as a mad bull.

Hearing Dad say there was a bee war on, though, made me curious—not to get anywhere near the battle, but to have a secret look. I watched for a chance to get away from Charlotte Ann, and pretty soon was peeking through the board fence that separates the chicken yard from the apiary; and there really *was* a war on this time, one of the hottest ones

I'd ever seen and heard. There was the sound of thousands of angry bees all over everywhere; and at the ramp of one of the hives, instead of there being several dozen dopey drones sleeping, there were scores of dead and dying bees piled all around the entrance.

I was glad I wasn't my father, who had to get a few pounds of honey to take to town to sell—even though he was getting it from a hive the farthest away from the thick of the battle.

While he was finishing getting the honey, I gathered the eggs for Mom to sell at the produce market in town, which would give her more grocery money.

Because something pretty important happened about the middle of the morning, I won't waste your reading time telling you about how many eggs my shadow and I found in the barn, hen house, and in different secret places where our old hens had sneaked away to lay their daily eggs.

My shadow went in and out with me, but not *up*. In maybe another year, though—or maybe even a month—she'd be able to climb the straight-up ladder leading from the barn's first floor to the haymow, and then we *would* have trouble. I'd have to tie her up like you do a dog, or she'd follow me up as far as she could, before she'd lose her grip and go tumbling down and crack her crown.

The eggs were gathered finally and in Mom's market basket in the house; I went back to work in the garden. I was thinning out the Scarlet Globe radishes; Dad was still in his bee veil robbing the bees of the honey they'd worked so hard for all spring and summer; and Charlotte Ann was, for a change, busy at the swing under the walnut tree, not fussing or whining, but actually sitting with her big, new, brunette, freckle-faced doll beside her on the wide board seat.

She wasn't big enough to do any chores around the place, but one thing we'd been letting her do for about a month was to get the mail when it came. Our mailman would stop his car near the gate and push the mail through the mesh into Charlotte Ann's chubby little hands, call her some kind of a nice name, such as "honey," or "sweetheart," wave a cheery good morning to any of the rest of the family that happened to be in sight, and go spinning down the pike toward Poetry's house, which was his next stop.

I didn't hear the mail coming and didn't see it either, since my head was lower than the tops of the Golden Bantam. When I straightened up to give my aching back a rest, I saw that Charlotte Ann had left the swing and was moseying around on the other side of the yellow rosebush in the yard, her new doll in one arm and the mail in the other.

The daily newspaper always had one comic strip I liked to read and one that was Mom's favorite, so I yelled to my shadow, "Come on with the mail! Hurry up!"

Her kind of half-cute answer was almost good enough to be in the paper. Her small, high-pitched voice came all the way across the rest of the yard with an answer that landed in my surprised ears and made me like her even better. "I *am* hurry-uppening!"

But she wasn't "hurry-uppening" fast enough, so I ran to meet her and was standing under the grape arbor reading the funnies, when Mom came out to look over my shoulder to read what was happening to Dagwood and Blondie and what Aunt Het thought about what was going on in the world.

Dad yelled from the apiary and asked if there were any letters for him. There weren't, and we all went back to our different jobs to get them done before we would have to eat dinner.

Well, as soon after dinner as she could, Mom got my shadow to sleep in the north bedroom, and away she and Dad went toward town. I watched our car as it stirred up a quarter-of-a-mile-long cloud of brown dust that moved with the lazy breeze out across the clover field to Bumblebee Hill. After it disappeared on the other side of the lane that leads to Little Jim's house, I plopped myself down on the board seat of the walnut tree swing to have a dreamy, lazy time baby-sitting until Charlotte Ann would wake up and start me on my topsy-turvy afternoon.

Nature was busy doing interesting things all around me. I let myself listen for a while to the different sounds, trying to hear more than I heard, and my mind's ear enjoyed it all. Every few seconds, a short-horned grasshopper would take off from the ground, rattle around in the air awhile, and plop down in another place. A robin whooped it up in the trees across the road, and a red squirrel saucily scolded about something or other, telling whatever he was mad at to go jump in the lake, or something.

In a sandy place at the base of the walnut tree beside me, I noticed five or six very small cone-shaped pits, which I knew had been dug by ant lions. At the bottom of each inch-deep pit, with all but its tiny head and jaws buried, was an ant lion larva waiting for a fly or some other

45

insect, such as an ordinary ant, to tumble accidentally in, and—presto!—like a fierce-fanged African lion, the larva would have a free breakfast or dinner or supper, depending on what time of day it was when its dinner came tumbling down into its homemade trap.

But as interesting as nature was to study and to think about, I'll have to admit I wasn't feeling very happy about not getting to meet with the gang at two o'clock under the Snatzerpazooka tree.

While I was still sitting and swinging, I tried to cheer myself up a little by quoting a poem called "The Swing," which I used to like when I was little, but it didn't help. All it did was remind me of what I wasn't going to get to do. The second stanza especially was hard on my nerves. That second stanza, as you probably know, goes like this:

> Up in the air and over the wall,
> Till I can see so wide,
> Rivers and trees and cattle and all,
> Over the countryside.

I couldn't see any wall, or cattle, or rivers, or even the countryside, from where *I* was sitting swinging.

I tried quoting the sentence our family had

enjoyed at garden time that morning, about the slumbering splendor in all of us that couldn't get out because of sin, and I said to myself, "Bill Collins, if there's any sleeping splendor inside you anywhere, you'd better do something about getting some of it out!"

Next I quoted to myself the Bible verse we'd had in Sunday school about honoring your father and your mother. It didn't make me feel any better, but it did calm me down a little. There was one thing I had made up my mind to do, and that was to obey God as long as I lived, even when I didn't feel like it, because He was always good to me and had loved everybody in the world enough to send His only Son to be punished for our sins.

I let my mind dream back through history to a time when the most important person there ever was had let Himself be nailed to a cross at a skull-shaped place called Golgotha.

All of a sudden, while I was feeling the wind in my face and the pleasant flapping of my shirt sleeves, as I whizzed back and forth, I got an idea that maybe every boy in the world ought to get. There wasn't a sin in the whole twenty-five thousand miles around the world He hadn't died for, and He hung on a cross on a hot afternoon under a scorching sun with nails driven all the way through his hands and feet.

It was a sad thought to think, and for a minute while I was talking to myself in my mind about it, it seemed like a boy named Bill Collins ought to try to be a better boy than he was.

Right then, I remembered the hot-tempered words I had said to Dad that morning; and without even realizing I was going to do it, I thought a quick, sad prayer for forgiveness, swallowed a lump in my throat, took a deep breath, and brought my swing to a stop. As soon as I was out, I moved stealthily across the yard toward an open screenless window to see how my sister was making out with her daily nap; she never wanted to go to bed by day any more than the boy in a certain poem, who said,

> In winter I get up at night
> And dress by yellow candlelight;
> In summer, quite the other way,
> I have to go to bed by day.

I got as far as the yellow rosebush in the middle of our side yard, when I heard one of the happiest sounds there ever is around Sugar Creek—a chattering and buzzing and talking and laughing, like a flock of blackbirds in autumn getting ready to fly South for the winter; it was the gang coming through the orchard to our house.

In a fleeting flash I was off to meet them. I swished past the cedar tree that grows not more than seventeen feet from our front door and Charlotte Ann's window, and was all the way out to the end of the hollyhocks in nothing flat. There I stopped, shaded my eyes from the two-o'clock sun, peered through the trees, and saw a flight of boys in different colored jeans and shirts, leap-frogging, tumbling over each other, climbing on and off each other's shoulders, laughing, and teasing.

Good old gang! I thought. *They're coming to have the meeting at my house instead of at the Snatzerpazooka tree!*

That afternoon while my folks were away, Charlotte Ann would have six baby-sitters instead of only one. Can you imagine that— six baby-sitters for one baby sister who couldn't be baby-sat with!

I leaped into action, and dashed like a streak of lightning through the gate between the two cherry trees and out into the orchard to shush them from all the noise they had been making. I warned them to keep still, or they'd wake up my shadow, and our afternoon would be upset.

"Yeah," Dragonfly chimed in, his popeyes

bulging a little and his crooked nose seeming a little more crooked than I'd ever noticed it before, "Let sleeping dogs lie!"

What he said and the way he said it stirred up my slumbering pride in my sister so that, without knowing I was going to say it, I said, "My sister is *not* a sleeping dog!"

What he said and what I answered made Charlotte Ann seem about seven times more wonderful than any boy's sister ever was. That goes to show that even though brothers and sisters sometimes fight with each other, they are ready to fight *for* each other the very minute one or the other of them is in trouble or needs any kind of help.

Dragonfly wasn't interested in what would maybe be a one-sided scuffle, so he said, "I'm sorry. She's really very pretty—for a girl, anyway," which spoiled his apology.

He made up for it by pulling a brand-new softball out of one of his pockets and saying, "Come on, everybody, let's play ball!"

Within the next hour, we had one of the most exciting experiences a gang of boys ever had—and some of it was even dangerous, especially to me.

4

Dragonfly's new softball was one of the finest I'd ever seen. He tossed it to me, and as I made a leap into the air and caught the ball with my bare right hand, I noticed how soft the waterproof, white rubber cover was.

I could hardly wait till we could get out into the barnyard to see how far I could knock it with my new softball bat—clear over Old Red Addie's pen and her apartment hog house, and maybe out into the south pasture.

Before leaving the yard, we decided to sneak a peek to see if my shadow, who had to go to bed by day, was still asleep.

Stealthily, we crept along from the yellow rosebush like Indian scouts scouting an enemy tribe, until we were just below the open window. Then, shushing each other with squinting eyes and with cautioning forefingers pressed to our lips, we sneaked six peeks and silently stole

51

away. Each of us had seen a tumble of soft-as-silk brown curls spread out on a pillow, a rag doll's right foot pressed against Charlotte Ann's nose, her pink rubber doll with its bashed-in forehead lying upside down on her stomach, her new large freckle-faced doll with its own brown hair spread out on one of Charlotte Ann's ankles, and, over in the corner, a two-foot-long brown-and-cream panda sitting up like it was his job to look after his sleeping mistress.

As soon as we had crawled far enough away to talk in whispers, Dragonfly all of a sudden rolled over on his back, closed his eyes and said to us, "What does my lying asleep like this remind anybody of? What legend that we studied in school last year?"

For a while, as Dragonfly lay there snoring with his eyes closed, and with a possum-like grin on his anything-but-handsome lopsided face, not a one of us said anything. Then he whined, "Can't anybody see anything that reminds him of anything?"

Poetry, in his squawking voice that was like the husky, rusty rustle of the tassels of the corn, said, "Looking down at you, seeing how sleepy you are, and knowing you haven't a thought in your empty head, reminds me of *The Legend of Sleepy Hollow*, by Washington Irving."

A minute after that, Poetry and Dragonfly were in a scuffle that started near the plum tree and lasted all the way across the lawn to the fence and to the tall grass that grew beside the gate near the mailbox. The reason for the rough-and-tumble scuffle was Poetry's answer to Dragonfly's question. I had been as surprised as anything with the answer myself—and several of the rest of us had thought it funny enough to let out a chorus of guffaws. Anybody could see that Dragonfly wanted one of us to say he reminded us of *Sleeping Beauty*.

It *was* funny, even though it was probably an old joke Poetry had read somewhere. You couldn't blame the rest of us for exploding with those noisy horselaughs. I saw a dark scowl come to life on Dragonfly's forehead, saw his thin jaw set, then the whole boy come to fast and furious spindle-legged life. He flopped his body over, grabbed Poetry around his ankles, and shoved himself up onto his own knees. Poetry went down like a tackled quarterback in a football game—and the rough-and-tumble scuffle was on.

Over and over and up and down and grunting and panting for breath and plop-plop-plopping over the grass, those two went to it while the rest of us rooted for both of them, forgetting we were baby-sitters. And then, as quick as it had started, the scuffle was history. Poetry, who with Dragonfly on the ground under him looked like a fat cowboy on a skinny horse, spied something in the tall grass near the mailbox post. Poetry grabbed for whatever it was and let out a squawking yell. "Hey! Look! Here's a letter to Bill Collins from Old Man Paddler!"

"Letter!" I exclaimed and made a dive for it, remembering a chubby-legged girl named Charlotte Ann, who that very morning had gotten the mail and had carried it all the way to the rosebush before I'd seen her. Carrying the letter with one hand and her large doll with the other, she had dropped the letter without knowing it, and it had been here all this time.

The letter's postmark was Santa Ana, California, where I knew the old man was having his vacation. It was addressed to "Bill Collins, secretary of the Sugar Creek Gang."

"Let me open it!" Little Jim begged. So did the rest. Big Jim said it was addressed to me and that nobody had a right to open anybody else's mail without permission, so in a few seconds, with ten eyes looking over my shoulders, I tore open one end of the long envelope—and what to twelve wondering eyes should appear but a sheaf of crisp, new, green one-dollar bills!

The money slipped out of my trembling hands and tumbled to the grass, where Circus quickly stooped and scooped the bills up. "Hey!" He exclaimed. "How come there are seven!"

"Yeah, how come?" Poetry panted, still short of breath from his scuffle with Dragonfly. "He was going to pay us a dollar apiece, and there are only six of us!"

We found out how come in a jiffy, when we read the letter. Just to be unselfish, I did let Big Jim read it—he was our leader and had ordered me to anyway. This is what, from the old man's careful trembling scrawl, Big Jim read.

Dear Boys:

You've made me very proud of you, the way you have looked after my place. When I read in the Sugar Creek *Times* how you not only helped capture the vandals but turned over your reward money to the Till family for Mother Till's hospital expenses, I realized how unselfish you really are.

I notice that one of the vandals is named Lawrence Bowen. That is the same name as a great grand nephew of Old Tom, the trapper. Old Tom, you know, used to live in the stone house you boys call the haunted house. Whenever you happen to think of it, just send up a silent prayer for him.

Big Jim stopped reading for a few seconds,

and I noticed he had a faraway look in his eyes, which meant that maybe right that very minute he was doing what Old Man Paddler had suggested. It wasn't exactly easy for me to do it too, because my mind was still hot at what the boys had done to the old man's place and what they had done to the gang itself, chopping a hole in our fishing boat, filling our spring reservoir with marsh mud, and even upsetting Old Man Paddler's wife's tombstone in the cemetery at the top of Bumblebee Hill.

While I was doing what Big Jim was maybe doing, I was also remembering something the old man had said to us quite a few times, "Boys don't need to be punished so much as they need to be changed." This, of course, made good sense and I knew *who* could change them.

Pretty soon Big Jim's mind came back to the letter, and he read on.

Because I have decided to stay out here two more weeks and enjoy the good fishing in the Pacific —caught seventeen mackerel and three bonitos yesterday from the barge five miles off shore— I'm sending your pay in advance. There'll be another dollar apiece when I get back. The seventh dollar in today's letter is to be used for having a new key made for the cabin's front door. I accidentally dropped mine overboard yesterday, and it is somewhere down in Davey Jones' locker at the bottom of the ocean. Use the key you have for a model, and hang the new one with the cave key you know where, so if I happen to come home in the middle of the night, I won't have to waken anybody to get into my house.

The Old man signed his letter like he always does, with only the initials *"O.M.P.,"* which as most anybody knows, means "Old Man Paddler."

Big Jim finished reading and was folding the letter, when Dragonfly broke in to say, "Look, there's something on the back side!" There was, and when we turned it over our twelve eyes began to read, "You boys are always interested in mysteries, so here is a new one for you. I had planned it for my return but now that I'm staying two more weeks, you may as well have it now."

A bright young boy, smart as a fox,
Studied a code and found a tin box;
And in the tin box, a treasure so rare,
Nor silver nor gold with its worth could compare.

Below the little four-line poem were three rows of letters. Just in case anybody reading this would like to get in on our secret, here is the code itself just as he printed it:

A B C D E F G H I J K L M N O P Q R S T U V W X Y Z
Z Y X W V U T S R Q P O N M L K J I H G F E D C B A

HZDWFHG   DLLWHSVW

57

"That doesn't make good sense," Dragonfly complained, proving he still didn't have a thought in his empty head.

"Sleepy Hollow," Poetry reminded him and for a few seconds it looked like there might be another scuffle.

Then Little Jim came up with an idea, saying, "The first row of letters is the ABC's forward, and the second row is the ABC's backward. Anybody want to hear me say 'em backward?"

With that, that little mouse-shaped face of a boy started in actually saying the ABC's backward without looking at the old man's letter. He got as far as NMLKJ, when Circus who as 'most anybody knows has six sisters and had to be smart just to stay alive, interrupted to suggest, "Maybe the first two lines of the letters are the code's *lock,* and the last line is the *key.* Fit the key into the lock, and you have the answer."

Well, for about thirty seconds—or maybe three or four minutes—we used our wits to see if we could figure out what the smart boy in the poem had already figured out so he could find the treasure in a tin box; then we gave up.

I wasn't interested right then in having another adventure of the mind, having had several already that day. An adventure of the *muscles* seemed more important, so as soon as we had all given up, I shoved the letter into my shirt pocket, and we went out into the barnyard to get our ball game started before anybody's noise could wake anybody up.

First, I went into the house to get my softball bat, and while I was there, I sneaked a peek to see if Charlotte was still asleep, and she still was; only, she had turned over, and her freckle-faced doll had probably turned over with her on account of it was now upside down. Glad that she was still asleep, I sneaked away and was quickly out with the gang again.

We had a fast meeting by the iron pitcher pump a few feet from the small water puddle the butterflies were making a white-and-yellow border around, and voted that I was to write a letter and send it airmail to thank the kind, long-whiskered old man for the seven pictures of George Washington on the seven one dollar bills and to tell him we'd use one of the dollars to pay to have a new cabin door key made for him and hide it in the secret place you know where.

That being decided, we broke up our meeting and were fast in the middle of an exciting ball game, having as much fun as six boys could have when they didn't dare let out a single excited yell on account of they didn't want a chubby little girl to wake up and come toddling out to upset everything.

Pretty soon, though, the fun *was* interrupted. Circus threw a fast ball to me while I was at bat. I saw it coming straight as an ivory white bullet. My muscles tightened; I swung back, and let go with a fierce, fast savage *wham,* that hit the ball square on the nose.

Say, that new rubber-covered softball shot off my bat like a rocket off a launching pad, sailed up into the barnyard sky, over the top of the chicken house, and like the arrow in Longfellow's poem, "it fell to earth I knew not where."

"Home run!" I yelled. Because I knew it'd take quite a while for anybody to field the ball and get it back onto our barnyard diamond, I made it a home walk instead of a home run, strutting proudly all the way around the tin-can bases.

Then is when our fun got interrupted. Poetry who had puffed his fat way around behind the chicken house to look for the ball, yelled over the roof to us, "Your ball's out here in the bee yard, and the bees are as mad as hornets!"

Dragonfly called back to Poetry, "Bill'll come and get it in a minute!"

But just because I was the son of an expert bee-handler did not mean I was going to risk my allergies in an apiary where a thousand bees were already stinging-mad at each other. I said so to the gang, but Dragonfly lowered his eyebrows at me and shot back, "It's *my* new ball, and *you're* the one that knocked the home run!"

"Come on and see for yourself why I can't go in to get it," I said to the gang.

Pretty soon we had worked our way around to the board fence with the wild grapevines sprawled all over it and were peeking over and through the leaves at the hives and the hot-tempered bees and also at the ivory white softball lying in the grass not more than thirty inches from the very hive, where this morning I'd seen dozens of wounded and dead bees piled all around the entrance and on the ramp leading to it. It was still like it had been, only a lot worse, with the dead and dying everywhere, like the Battle of Gettysburg you read about in history books. You could also smell the odor of bee venom hanging in the air like the smell of smoke on a damp day.

"Smell that bee venom?" I said to

everybody. "There's a bee battle on. A robber swarm is stealing honey, and they're all stinging each other. They smell the poison from their own stings, and that makes them still madder. It's like committing suicide to go in there to try to get that ball! Besides, I had onions for dinner and I'm sweating all over from playing so hard!"

"What's *that* got to do with it?" Dragonfly, still the spokesman, demanded.

"Plenty," I said back. "Different smells such as onion breath, perfume, or body sweat make a mad bee still madder. *Look out! Duck!*" I ordered. "They've located us!"

And they had—two or three of them had, anyway. We dropped to the ground like six dead ducks, waited till the angry bees left us, and then we crawled back to the barnyard again to our baseball diamond.

"They'll be calmed down by tonight," I said, "I'll sneak in and get the ball while they sleep." But Dragonfly wouldn't give up. "I don't want a thousand bees swarming all over and stinging my ball!" he fussed. Then without anybody even calling a meeting, he cried, "It's been moved and seconded that Bill put on his father's bee veil and go in and get the ball! All in favor say aye."

I for some reason, was the only one to vote no. I tried to be funny by saying, "Five of the eyes see it but one is already swollen shut."

"Chicken!" Poetry, my best friend up to now, said to me.

"Yeah, chicken!" Dragonfly copy-catted him, and Circus, who sometimes has better judgment than the rest, looked at me with accusing eyes. Even Big Jim's grin told me he thought I wasn't brave enough to go and get an innocent ball.

Now, as any boy knows, anybody doesn't like to be called "chicken," which means whoever calls him that thinks he's a scaredy-cat.

But I happened to remember some sharp advice from my father when he had said to me, "Son, no boy likes to be thought a coward, but it's better to have good sense than it is to be brave, better to be *thought* a fool than it is to *be* one."

Only Little Jim seemed to be on my side. He piped up to say, "With so many bees on the ground all around the ball, Bill might step on some of them—and who wants to smash a helpless honeybee!"

"Yeah," I grabbed onto his idea and agreed,

"Who does! Dad is very particular about what happens to any of his bees!"

"Listen, you guys," I then thought of to say, "did anybody hear Charlotte Ann crying or calling or fussing or anything?"

But nobody had.

Right then something happened that made me realize how stubborn our crooked-nosed, spindle-legged member of the gang really was. "All right," he said with a set jaw, "if you're going to be a chicken, I know a boy who's *not* chicken!"

With that, that little set-willed rascal of a popeyed boy swung around and started on the run for our toolshed, letting fly back over his thin shoulder, "If your *father* can do it, I can do it!"

I knew what he now had on his one-track mind to do. He was going to get my father's bee veil, and go into a lion's den of ten thousand angry bees, and it was about the most foolish thing a boy could ever do! Of all people in the world, a boy who never knew when he was going to get an asthma attack ought not to let himself get stung maybe seventeen times. He might be even more allergic to bee venom than I was.

I was off and after him in a fast-footed jiffy,

catching up with him just as he was yanking open the toolshed door.

"Look!" I said to him. "You'd be absolutely crazy to go out there now!"

He wormed out of my grasp and made a dive for Dad's hat with the long veil on it, just as I made a dive for him, caught him behind by the belt of his jeans, and pulled him back.

We scuffled a minute—or a half minute, anyway—and what might have happened next is anybody's guess, but all of a sudden that little guy began to cry, "I've *got* to get it back, my father'll clobber me if I don't!"

Well, to make this part of the story shorter, this is what, in the next few jiffies, with Drangonfly and I outside the toolshed door and standing under the grape arbor, I found out, "I'm being punished for something I did yesterday," he confessed. "My parents told me I couldn't play with my new ball for two days, and it was on the top of the tall kitchen cabinet right where I could see it but couldn't have it! They've gone to town to get groceries, and they'll be home by four o'clock, and if the ball's not up there, I'll get the daylights whammed out of me!"

And that was another that. My wristwatch told me it was already almost three o'clock. If we wanted to help Dragonfly, we'd have to get the ball in a hurry—and I, Bill Collins, son of an expert bee-handler, who was scared of even ordinary bees around a hive, was going to have to forget about it being better to have good sense than it was to be brave.

I knew what I was going to have to do—get Dad's bee veil, which I'd never worn in my life, put on his gloves, and risk getting stung maybe seventeen times. I knew it, because I knew Dragonfly's father had an extra hot temper, and it didn't seem right for a member of our own gang, even though he had done wrong, to have to get the daylights punished out of him like I'd seen happen to him several times before.

*   *   *

I was surprised at how well I could see through the mosquito netting when I had Dad's hat and veil on. It was sort of like looking through the lace curtains at our living room window. The ends of the long veil were tucked into the collar of my Leatherette jacket, which I usually wore only in the winter, but I knew the bees couldn't sting through it.

A few seconds later, I said, "Well, here goes nothing!" My voice sounded brave, but I was trembling inside and maybe as afraid as I'd ever been in my half-long life because I was remembering the time I'd been stung five times all at once and not only had gotten sick at the stomach but had almost fainted. Of course a thing like that *couldn't* happen to anybody who had his veil and bee gloves on—or could it?

I sneaked around to the apiary gate, pushed it open, and also *left* it open, just in case I might have to come rushing out in a hurry.

Through the veil I could see five heads of five boys peering over and through the leaves of the wild grapevine that smothered the board fence. I worked my way along on hands and knees for a while, until I happened to think there might be a dead or a dying or a very-much-alive bee—or a half dozen—in the grass from the fierce, fast-buzzing bee battle they were having.

The closer I got to the hives where the battle was, the more I smelled the bee venom, and the more I realized it would never have done for Dragonfly to have done what I was doing.

Now I could see the ball, half hidden in the tallish blue grass. If I could get safely to within a few feet, I'd make a wild dive for it, scoop it up in one of my gloved hands, toss it over the board fence, and run like Peter Rabbit with Mr. McGreggor after him, straight for the open gate, and lose myself among the long-hanging branches of the trees in the orchard.

The angry buzzing was so loud, I could hardly hear myself think, as I crept nearer, hoping the bees wouldn't smell my onion breath or the perspiration I'd been perspiring in the ball game.

What an angry buzzing!

And then, just as I was within maybe twenty feet of the hive where the battle was on, and had the ball in plain sight, I heard something else.

It was a sound that sent shivers all over me and up and down my spine. I was seeing as well as hearing, and *what* I saw was Charlotte Ann Collins, toddling happily along, with her large freckle-faced doll in her arms coming straight through the wide-open bee yard gate to be where her brother was, without having any sense at all of the danger she was in.

Well, as you maybe remember, there is a line in a certain poem that says, "I have a little shadow that goes in and out with me."

My shadow right that minute had followed me in, and she was going to have to get *out* in a hurry—with or without me!

In my mind's eye I saw a whole lot more than I saw through the bee veil. I saw that little rascal of a kid sister wake up in her bed and, hearing all the noise we had been making, decide she wanted to be where we all were,—that's what a toddler her age likes to do more than anything else anyway, like a little monkey does the same things it sees others do.

And now here she was, walking innocently toward the hot center of the battle of the bee yard.

What on earth! my worried mind exclaimed to me.

"Get Back!" I yelled to my baby sister. "You'll get the living daylights stung out of you! *Back! Don't come any closer!"*

But what do you suppose that little rascal of a brown-haired, very-pretty-faced, happy-go-lucky, dumbbell of a girl kept on doing?

Already inside, she kept on coming toward me, dragging her doll by one arm and grinning like she didn't have a worry in the world. What was her veiled brother so excited about on such a beautiful sunshiny day?

5

What *was* I so excited about?

If you have ever been in a situation like the one I was in, you'll know that I had about seventeen thousand, six hundred and forty-three savage little stingers all around me, all of them fighting mad, and looking for anything and anybody they didn't like.

One selfish hive of bees had decided to try to steal honey from their next-door neighbor rather than wear out their wings in the fields and trees, gathering pollen from one flower after another and carrying it miles and miles home and storing it away. All they had to do, they probably thought—if bees can think—was to sneak into their neighbors' hive and help themselves.

The only thing was, the neighbors had worked hard for their honey, and they weren't going to have any thieves break into their hives in broad daylight and rob their honey bank.

And so the battle was on, and those seventeen thousand bees were as mad as hornets. Anything or anybody that got in the way was going to get stung.

Two things were in the way right that minute — three rather — a new, ivory white softball that probably smelled like it had been handled by six boys' sweaty hands, one boy with a bee veil on, and one chubby-legged—*bare*-legged—happy-go-lucky, innocent-faced, three-year-old, brown-haired little girl heading straight for the thick of the battle.

I let out another yell—and another and another—and started waving my arms and running toward Charlotte Ann, ordering her, *"I said get out of here! Run for your life!"*

With my right gloved hand, I quickly scooped up the ball, which had maybe nineteen bees all over it, tossed it up and over the board fence where five boys were, and lit out for Charlotte Ann, taking with me and around me and all over me as many bees as were already all around and all over me.

Now, I ask you, what do you do at a time like that?

What do you do?

To get my mind in even more of a whirlwind than it was, five pairs of lungs on the other side of the board fence started yelling different orders.

Anybody with even half as much sense as I didn't seem to have right then, would have known I was making a mistake, taking all those bees with me where I was going. I myself, wouldn't get stung on my face and neck on account of the veil I had on. The gloves would protect my hands, and my heavy jacket and jeans would protect the rest of me, but Charlotte Ann didn't have on any protection.

One nonsensical idea that came to me, as I dashed toward the gate and the cutest little sister a boy ever had, was what Dragonfly's scared voice had called out for me to do, and that was, "Take off your veil and put it on *her!*"

Poetry, who nearly always had a keen mind in an emergency, called, *"Drop flat!* They'll wonder what happened and'll buzz around all over above where your head was and you'll be saved."

"I don't need to be saved!" I yelled. "I'm already safe! I'm trying to save Charlotte Ann!"

But of course, you don't save any three-year-old, happy-go-lucky little sister from getting stung half-to-death by taking a swarm of mad bees toward her as fast as you can run!

Right then, in the middle of all that excited yelling and screaming and angry buzzing—and noise and worry—there was a blurred flurry of something else happening. I heard it almost before I saw it start to happen—and then I *really* saw.

Our acrobat, the boy who could climb trees quicker than any other member of the gang, who had muscles like steel, who could run faster than any of the rest of us, and jump higher and farther, shot up and over that board fence like a boy doing a pole vault in a track meet. Like a streak of blue-jeaned lightning, Circus was out in the middle of the apiary, arrowing his way to the gate near where Charlotte Ann still was. Quicker'n a cat's claw striking out at a dog in a fight, Circus scooped up that innocent-faced, dumbbell of a sister of mine and galloped with her toward the low-hanging branches of the Maiden-blush apple tree. The second he was under, he dropped to the ground with Charlotte Ann under him, spreading his arms out over her like a mother hen spreads her wings over her chick.

Even while I was seeing all that excitement through the mosquito netting of Dad's veil, there went racing through my mind part of a sermon I'd heard in the Sugar Creek Church. On a sad day, the one who had come to save the world had stood looking down at the city of Jerusalem, and said, "Oh Jerusalem, Jerusalem. How often would I have gathered you as a hen gathers her chickens under her wings—" something like that.

The bees were still landing on me from all around me, whamming into my hat and veil and arms and shoulders, and the noise was like a cyclone tearing along through Harm Groenwald's south clover field.

Like a scared cottontail with a pack of hounds after him, I raced through that open apiary gate and into the orchard, heading off to the left so I wouldn't be carrying any bees toward Circus and Charlotte Ann, running buzzetv-sizzle for the low branches of the Jonathan apple tree at the edge of the blackberry patch. Quicker'n a scared flash, I was under and lying panting on the ground—and also wincing, and grunting, on account of I had landed on maybe seven hard windfall apples.

I lay there holding my onion breath and waiting till the bees decided I was dead—or wasn't worth wasting a lot of good stingers on—and went back to a more interesting fight. Then I came out into the peaceful world of sunlight and hurried to where Circus and Charlotte Ann were, a safe distance away from the battlefield, and not far from the end of the row of hollyhocks which were still saying to me, "Ambition, Bill Collins! Don't be a lazy good-for-nothing. Don't be a drone, lying around the front of a beehive."

"Will you shut up!" I all of a loud-voiced sudden cried in the direction of those tall, beautiful flower stalks.

"Will *who* shut up?" Big Jim demanded, and Circus answered, "She can't help crying; she got stung on her arm."

Of course Charlotte Ann was crying. What little girl wouldn't, at a time like that!

I quick had Dad's hat and veil and gloves off and was focusing my eyes on Charlotte Ann's chubby little arm just below her dimpled elbow, and sure enough she had been stung. She wasn't crying very loud, but was sobbing in her throat, and actually seemed to be trying to keep from being a scaredy-cat.

Well, I knew from things I'd read that even one sting was nothing to be sneezed at and ought to be treated right away; so right away I was on the run for the house, to the medicine cabinet to get the special bee ointment we had there.

And that's when I ran into trouble. The medicine cabinet was *locked,* which is a precaution our family had taken on account of it isn't good to have any medicines where a small child can get them and poison herself.

I looked in the secret place where we kept the key, and it wasn't there! I kept on looking around in different places, and still couldn't find the key. Now I could hear Charlotte Ann really crying out there by the pump, and calling me.

What, I wondered, was somebody trying to do to her? For that was the way it sounded, like somebody was hurting her.

I got there just in time to see Dragonfly with a pair of pliers that looked like Dad's, ready to use them on Charlotte Ann's arm.

"Hey!" I yelled, as the screen door slammed behind me and as I dashed down the steps out onto the boardwalk to the pump, "Let my sister alone!"

"The stinger!" Dragonfly defended himself. "It's still in! I was only going to pull it out!"

That's when I was glad I was a bee-handler's son. My Dad had taught me something everybody ought to know about honeybee stings.

"That stinger's full of poison," I said to anybody who was interested in hearing it. "A bee stinger is shaped like a barbed blade, and its barbs catch into your flesh like a fishhook. Sometimes the bee gets stuck onto your arm or back or wherever it happens to sting you, and can't get away without tearing loose.

"When it does tear loose—here, give me that pair of pliers!" I had to talk sharply to that little stubborn, spindle-legged member of the gang, or he'd have still used the pliers on the stinger, and it'd have been like squeezing on a squeeze bottle of liquid detergent. He'd have squeezed into Charlotte's already swelling arm all the poison that was left in the stinger.

As soon as I had stopped Dragonfly, I asked Poetry for his knife.

"Knife!" different voices cried out to me. "You're going to *cut* it out? Going to cut a hole in your sister's arm?"

Remembering I was going to be a doctor someday, I said as calmly as I could, "When a bee tears loose, he leaves his stinger behind, also the sheath the stinger was in, which is a part of the bee, and he leaves his whole sackful of poison."

And right then I began to feel fine. I was a doctor now, I was going to perform an operation, and all the rest of the gang were just interns watching—and maybe taking orders from me to help me.

"Like this," I said, remembering how Dad had done it to three of the five stingers I'd been stung with a month ago, only three of them having been left in my flesh. I was going to use the knife blade to carefully scrape the stinger loose *without* any of the rest of the poison being squeezed out.

"All right, girl patient!" I said. "We'll be through in just a minute." I got my left hand under her arm, and with the knife blade loosened the stinger; just like that, there it was, lying on the pink skin of the fast-swelling arm, with part of the bee still fastened to it.

"Now," I said to Dragonfly, "I'll take the pliers." With them, I picked up the stinger, holding it up for them all to see.

Little Jim let out a gasp then, and said, "No wonder you didn't want to use the pliers on it. Look at that little drop of poison on the end!"

Charlotte Ann had stopped crying and was watching now through her tears, like it was somebody else's arm that had been operated on. But I could tell there was still a lot of pain, and I wished I could find our cabinet key, so I could get the ointment. It was Little Jim that came up

78

with what sounded like a good idea. "Remember," he said, "when we killed the old mother bear, we had her cub for a week? When he got stung all over his nose, he went down to the spring and made his own medicine out of clay and patted it on his nose?"

That, I thought, made sense. If a baby bear used a clay pack to take the pain and maybe even the swelling out of beestings, then why not use clay for a baby human being?

"Here, kid," I said to my sister. "We'll make you some nice, clean, brown medicine out of clay from the very pretty butterfly puddle."

But *Kid* had an idea of her own. Like a lively night crawler wriggling out of a boy's hand to keep from being put on a fishhook, Charlotte Ann was out of my grasp and scooting like a scared squirrel for the grape arbor and Mom's flowerpot table, with her doctor-brother in fast pursuit.

Right then, I had what a storywriter calls a "flashback." I, the doctor, had been in the middle of my operation, and my patient who up to now had been patient, had stopped being that and was running away.

The flashback was of a time when Charlotte Ann, like 'most any boy's sister, had been making mud pies with the mud in that very same water puddle by the iron pitcher pump—even after Mom had ordered her not to play there anymore. One day Charlotte Ann, all dressed up for Sunday school, had disobeyed, accidentally lost her balance, and fallen— *kersplash*—into the puddle, and her fresh, crisp, yellow dress, in which she had never looked prettier, went down with her. Talk about excitement around our place—most of it was in Mom's ordinarily quiet mind! There was spattered mud and muddy water all over the yellow dress and a pair of black patent leather shoes, When Mom both saw and heard what had happened, her temper came to life, and she went into motherly action. Several minutes later, when she put the beech switch back on the lower horns of the gun rack, her face was very sad, like she had done something she shouldn't have.

As you maybe know, that was one of the hardest things my mother ever had to do — actually punish either one of her two children—although for some reason it seemed a little easier for her to punish her son than her daughter.

Mom was sad almost all the rest of that whole day, on account of her having such a tender heart. Well, after that switching,

Charlotte Ann had stayed away from the puddle—though many a time I'd seen her standing three feet from it, watching the butterflies having the time of their lives there, and maybe wondering how come a very pretty butterfly with white or yellow wings could play in a water puddle and a human being couldn't.

That, while I was giving chase to my chubby-legged runaway sister, was the flashback.

But a doctor in the middle of an operation can't let his patient get up and leave the surgery room, so I kept on giving chase, and she kept on running. I'd have caught her in a few fast leaps, if I hadn't stumbled over one of Mom's flowerpots I'd been ordered to pick up and had forgotten to and had fallen head over heels.

When I finally caught my patient, she was as far as the mailbox near the front gate. I quickly swooped her up and carried her, wriggling and fussing, back toward the outdoor operating room.

We *had* to get a little clay pack on her beesting, *had* to! "Listen," I tried to explain to her, as we struggled along past the plum tree to where my five interns were waiting, "I'm *not* going to hurt you. I'm trying to *help* you!"

But she couldn't be explained to. So I kept

on carrying her thirty-two wriggling pounds, until we got to the pump, where she did let me put cold water on her red arm.

"See?" I said to her. "I'm not going to hurt you. I'm going to put something that looks like cold, black licorice candy on you." I winked to Poetry who had a small clay pack already made.

He came up behind me, slipped it into my hand and—well *that's* when it happened. We were too close to the puddle—and Charlotte Ann had too good eyesight not to see. She probably saw more than she saw—not just a small, cool clay pack in a boy's hand, but herself getting a switching with a beech switch.

Anyway before I realized what was going on, she was out of my grasp again and starting to start toward the barnyard baseball diamond, stumbled over a hat with a bee veil on it and down she went, clean dress, hair ribbon and all, into the puddle, the hat and veil getting there first and landing in the puddle with her.

But that wasn't all that was going on. I heard from some direction or other, the sound of a motor, looked up and out to the walnut tree just in time to see a long green car with two people in it, stopping at the gate.

"My parents!" I cried to all of us. "My folks are home!"

As you can very well imagine, my father wouldn't have a very hard time seeing a lot more than he saw. Right in front of his eyes was a bee hat lying on its crown in the butterfly puddle, a smoker on the pump platform, a broken flowerpot on its side beside Mom's flower table, six boys' worried faces; and if he had looked beyond the chicken house, he might have seen an apiary gate wide open, and several old hens gobbling up grains, greens, grubs, and grit on their way in; also, right in front of his eyes was his own daughter standing crying with the front of her dress and her hands and knees spattered with mud.

Right then there was plenty to *hear:* Charlotte's worried sobbing, six boys trying to explain things, and my mother's astonished voice crying from the pump platform, where all of a sudden she was, "Bill Collins! What on earth is going on here! What have you boys been doing to that child!"

But nobody answered — not right then, 'cause something else started to happen.

Mom got a scared look on her face and I heard her cry out, "Circus! What's the matter!"

I quickly looked in the direction where our

acrobat was standing under the grape arbor, and saw him turn as pale as a ghost and start gasping for breath.

"The bees!" he rasped, "They stung me all over—my shoulder—and arms and—" He doubled up then like he was in terrible pain in his stomach, and our curly-headed acrobat of a wonderful guy, who had leaped over our board fence like a cowboy at a rodeo leaping from his horse to tie up a roped calf, and had swooped up my sister and carried her to safety, spreading his arms out over her to protect her from getting stung, that wonderful quick-thinking member of our gang slumped to the ground like a sack of wheat.

6

And that was another that—a *frightening* that, that was enough to scare anybody who didn't know what to do, half out of what few wits he might have had at the time.

It was my Dad who was a bee-handler and well-read on what to do in an emergency like that, who leaped into fast first-aid action.

"Mother!" he, the new doctor who had taken over in a new and really serious case, ordered his nurse, "get the nebulizer— *quick!* Bill, you call Dr. Gordon! We've got a case of anaphylactic shock on our hands!"

I cut in to say to Mom, "The medicine cabinet key's lost—I couldn't find it."

But Mom was already on her way, digging into her handbag as she hurried up the boardwalk to the house.

I didn't find out till afterward that they'd taken the key to town with them to have another key made, so in case one got lost we'd have a spare.

Mom was in and out of the house with a flurry of skirts, coming back to where we were with the nebulizer and a pillow, letting the screen door slam behind her like a boy in a hurry, and in a few fast seconds, the new doctor and the new nurse, with six interns watching saw some of the finest skill in first aid anybody ever saw.

It was then that I realized what thoughtful parents I really had. They not only knew what to do for anybody who went into a state of what Pop called *anaphylactic shock* from beestings, but they also had emergency medication ready.

In the nebulizer, which I noticed was like the one Dragonfly used sometimes when he had an asthma attack, was a special medicine which I learned later—and also learned how to spell—was *epinephrine*. They quickly had Circus's head on the pillow in Mom's lap and were helping him inhale some of the fine fog that came out of the nebulizer everytime Dad squeezed the bulb.

It seemed like Dr. Gordon was a long time in coming, but in less than ten minutes, he came racing down the road in a cloud of dust.

Circus was breathing better before the

doctor with his bag came striding past the high swing at the walnut tree, across the yard to where we all were. He gave his patient some kind of a shot in the arm; and then while our acrobat, still as pale as a sick white cat lay with his head on Mom's pillow in her lap, he started in treating seven fast-swelling beestings on Circus's arms and shoulders—the stings Circus had gotten instead of my wonderful little sister.

When the doctor glanced down at his wristwatch, I noticed it was almost four o'clock.

Dragonfly must have come to then, 'cause I saw his scared dragonfly-like eyes on the wristwatch too, and I knew he was seeing more than he was seeing. He was maybe thinking that if *my* folks had already come home from shopping, his might be home, too, and he'd better get there in nothing flat to get his softball back up on top of the kitchen cabinet where it was supposed to have stayed for two days, and hadn't. And *if* it had we wouldn't have played ball with it, I wouldn't have knocked a home run, the ball wouldn't have landed in the middle of a bee battle, and we wouldn't have had all the trouble we were in.

Like a spindle-legged arrow, he was off across the yard toward the still-open gate, racing like a fox with a hound after it for the Gilbert house—Gilbert being his last name, just in case you might have forgotten.

It seemed also to most of the rest of the gang that it was time for them to go home, too, which it was.

The doctor himself decided to drive Circus home, while Mom phoned his mother part of what had happened and to prepare her for the news, and maybe keep her from getting some kind of shock when she saw the doctor driving into their place with their only son.

In only a little while, the Collins family was alone—each one with his own thoughts, mine especially being the kind I get sometimes when I know I've done something wrong and can't be sure what until my folks tell me.

It was like the quiet after a storm, and I could hardly believe my ears when I heard Mom say kindly to Charlotte Ann, "Come on, dear, we'll get cleaned up and your dress changed. You can wear you new *pink* dress the rest of the day."

"She got stung by a bee," I started to explain, "and we were trying to give her first aid. I was just going to put on a little clay from the puddle there, and—"

"You accidentally put on too much?" Dad asked with a very strange tone of voice.

"That's it," I said. "It was an accident."

"I see also that you put a little first aid on my bee hat."

If it had been the right time to be funny I'd have said, "Well, *it* got stung, *too*, you know. The bees stung it instead of me!" But anything funny right then wouldn't have seemed funny, so I swallowed my thoughts and stared at Dad's hat; it was still on its crown in the water puddle, and several butterflies were fluttering around above it like yellow and white flowers with winged petals.

"Before you begin," my grim-faced father said to me, "I want to tell you that I'm going to believe everything you say and accept your story exactly as you tell it. A thing like this couldn't happen all by itself. You run and get the groceries first and carry them into the house."

I stared at him, wondering if I was hearing right—especially his very kind tone of voice.

"Go on," he said, "get the groceries and take them into the kitchen, and we'll talk later."

I went toward the car for the groceries. When I came back, I stopped at the kitchen door, and asked Dad, "Do I *have* to take them in?"

"You do," he said. He opened the screen for me and I went inside where Mom and Charlotte Ann were, wishing there would be some kind of veil a boy could wear to keep from getting stung with what would probably be some very sharp words.

It seemed like when I walked into our kitchen with the large grocery sacks in my arms, that I expected a swarm of words to come flying at me from wherever Mom was. Instead, Mom wasn't even in the kitchen, but was in the bathroom with Charlotte Ann, and my sister was giggling like she was having the most fun a child could ever have

I understood why Charlotte Ann was so tickled when I heard Mom say, "Here we go! Off with the wing feathers! In just a minute now we'll have the whole pheasant skinned."

It was the same trick Dad used on Charlotte Ann every evening in the summer, when he was fooling her into thinking it was fun to go to bed by day. He played a game with her, pretending she was a pheasant, and he was skinning her; and Charlotte Ann would be out of her day clothes into her night ones in only a few jiffies, without realizing what had happened.

"Sing the 'pillar song," I heard Charlotte Ann say.

And Mom sang it to her—the one you already know about, on account of I had sung it to her myself that very day.

It seemed I ought to take advantage of Mom's good humor, which might not be so good if she happened to see or hear her son in the kitchen, so I very quietly set the grocery sacks on the table, and crept like a striped caterpillar to the door and went out shutting the kitchen screen door more quietly than I had in a long time. When I reached the iron pitcher pump, Dad was just closing the apiary gate. He turned and came toward me, carrying Charlotte Ann's freckle-faced doll.

"I'm terribly sorry," I began, but Dad cut in to say, "That's all right, you don't have to apologize. Just tell the story as it happened."

His kind voice was like a boy's hand stroking a kitten, so it was easy for me to tell him everything you already know—about the baseball game, how we were playing with Dragonfly's ball which he wasn't supposed to have taken off the top of their kitchen cabinet for another day, and we had been right in the middle of a lot of fun when I knocked the home run.

When I got that far, Dad cut in again to say, "Home run! That's fine! Where'd the ball go—how far?"

"That's what started the trouble," I told him. "I knocked it all the way over the top of the chicken house, and it landed in the bee yard, whamming into one of the hives the war was on in, and because in a little while Dragonfly would have to go home and put the ball back where he wasn't supposed to have taken it from, somebody *had* to go in and get it.

"They called me chicken, and I couldn't stand that. But I wouldn't have gone, if I hadn't wanted to keep him from getting clobbered by his hot-tempered father. He has a very hot-tempered father."

"So, you decided to do your good turn for the day—help Roy deceive his parents!"

"No, sir," I said to Dad. "I knew it was wrong, but I still didn't want him to get the kind of licking his father gives. His father whips too hard," I finished with a little worried hope in my voice, on account of my mind was in the toolshed looking at three beech switches on the lower horns of the gun rack.

"Well," I went on, "I was scared—and you know how scared I am of the bee yard. That's why I borrowed your veil, and also why I left the gate open so I could get out in a hurry.

"I hadn't any sooner crept around to where I could get the ball, than I heard and saw Charlotte Ann coming toward the open gate.

"I yelled to her to stay back and she wouldn't, but came on dragging her freckle-faced doll by the arm. That's when I forgot there were seventy bees all around my veil as mad as hornets, and started toward her, yelling and ordering her to go back and accidentally taking all those bees with me.

"And that's when Circus leaped like an antelope over the board fence and rushed across the bee yard, scooped Charlotte Ann up, and carried her out into the orchard, and under the branches of the Maiden-blush apple tree; and that's also how come he got stung seven times on the arms and shoulders and how come Charlotte Ann got stung only once.

"The bee that stung Charlotte Ann on the arm, had left his stinger in, so I scraped it off with Poetry's knife, like you taught me how to do. When I couldn't find the medicine cabinet key, we decided to put clay on it so it wouldn't swell so much and would quit hurting. But Charlotte Ann remembered the switching Mom had given her for getting herself all spattered with mud, so—well, she tried to run away from the doctor, and the doctor ran after her and brought her back to the operating table and—then you came home."

All this time Dad and I had been standing under the crossbeam of the grape arbor, not more than nine feet from the beech switches in the toolshed. I had made the story a little longer so in case there was a hot temper inside my father, it would have a chance to cool off a little.

"That, son," Dad astonished me by saying, "is a very satisfactory explanation—a little long, perhaps, but as I told you awhile ago, I'm going to accept it.

"Now I think we'd better get started on the rest of the garden before chore time. Did you find enough fish worms to go fishing?"

What on earth! I thought. And without planning to, I said, "Aren't you going to give me a licking?"

Dad pumped himself a drink of water, handed me one first, saying, "Why should I? Why punish a boy for thinking? You did just right, son! I'm proud of you! I'm not sure I could have done any better."

All of a sudden it was a wonderful sunshiny afternoon, and my heart was as light as a feather in a whirlwind.

I guess maybe there isn't a thing in the world that feels better to a boy than when he and his father are forgiven to each other, and there is a twinkle in his eye like he likes you and thinks you are even better than you hope you are.

Right away my biceps ordered me to skin a cat on the crossbeam above my head. I was up and over and skinning it in a split second. Then I swung my whole body up and sat on the crossbeam, started to flap my arms and crow, when Dad said to me, "Something fell out of your shirt pocket."

"That," I looked down at what he had in his hands and said, "is a letter from Old Man Paddler. It came this morning."

Being interrupted like that, I forgot to crow, and came down fast.

Right then Mom came out the back door, Charlotte Ann in her new pink dress was with her. That little sister of mine was grinning like everything, and holding her arm out for me to see, saying *"Ban'age!* I got a ban'age!"

I looked at the place on her arm where the bee had stung her and Mom had tied a white bandage on it—a "ban'age" being something I remembered Charlotte Ann was always proud to wear. Sometimes she would want one on when there wasn't anything wrong at all.

"Look!" Mom explained cheerfully, lifting her face and stretching her neck in the direction of the south pasture. "There goes a whirlwind!"

I looked where she was looking and saw a funnel of dust and grass and leaves circling crazily along in the middle of the south pasture coming toward the walnut tree.

It seemed like a good time to change any subject my folks might want to start talking about, so I said, "If you like it and want it, I'll go catch it and bring it back for you!"

I was off with nobody stopping me, heading bareheaded for the pasture bars near the barn, scooting through and like a streak racing out into the middle of one of the happiest sights a boy ever sees out in the country.

It's not an easy thing to do—stay in the center of a whirlwind which never knows itself which way it's going, nor how long it is going to live. I hadn't any sooner than felt the whirlwind's wind in my face and all over me and around me, than as quick as scat it had scattered itself into nothing, and I was running in circles like a chicken with its head off. The only wind there was was what I myself was making—which is what a whirlwind does. It starts out of nowhere, lives a very excited life for a few minutes, and then quick as a boy can skin a cat on a grape arbor crossbeam—the wind in it dies, and the whirlwind is gone like a burst soap bubble.

My heart was still as light as a straw in a whirlwind when I pushed myself through the pasture bars on the way back—walking from the barn to where Mom and Dad were, with my shadow running toward me, stumbling along in different directions not watching where she was going, on account of she was looking down at her arm, holding it up for me to see and saying "Ban'age! I got a ban'age!"

And do you know what? It was almost worth all the worried excitement we had been having for the past hour, just to see how happy that white gauze *ban'age* made that cute little shadow that goes in and out and up and down and 'round and 'round with me.

A worried thought came to my mind then. What if Dragonfly hadn't gotten home in time to get his baseball back on the kitchen cabinet before his folks got back from town!

I found out a few minutes later. My shadow and I were all the way to the water puddle, which she walked away out around for some reason, when I heard the phone ring two longs and a short short, and right away heard Mom's voice answer it.

"Who is it?" I called in through the east window, where I was, almost before Mom could get to the phone from inside of the house.

I felt fine when Mom answered out through the window to me, "It's Roy. He wants to know if we saw his parents in town anywhere. They aren't home yet."

That *really* made me feel fine, 'cause I knew that now there wasn't a one of the gang that would be missing tomorrow when we went up to Old Man Paddler's cabin to spend the night—except maybe Circus, who might still not be feeling well from so many beestings.

What a wonderful time we are going to have!

As we always do when we spend the night on a hike or a camping trip, we would lie awake in the dark before going to sleep, tell ghost stories, laugh and talk about different things boys like to talk about, it being almost as important for boys to be mischievous and talk to boys as it is for women to talk to women.

Dad and I dived into the chores almost right away, since Mom wanted an early supper. "There's just one thing about tomorrow night," I said to Dad while he and I were washing up at the round-topped table near the iron pitcher pump.

"One thing, what?" he said, through the towel he was drying his face with.

"What if we accidentally stumble onto a wild animal of some kind up there in the hills? Remember we had to kill a bear a few years ago—and we also killed a wildcat. Maybe a boy ought to take his rifle along! Don't you think—"

My back was to the kitchen door while I was talking, and I was looking longingly through the toolshed door at the middle horns of the gun rack.

Dad's smothered voice stopped me with a cautious "Shh."

I shushed just in time to see behind me out of the corner of my eye, my mother standing in the open door, and I knew why Dad had stopped me.

I didn't even need to hear him explain a jiffy later, "You *do* want to go, don't you?"

"Sure," I said, "but—"

"Then soft-pedal the talk about bears and wildcats!"

We went in then to supper and to a happy family around the table. Twenty-four hours from now the gang would be in the middle of a new and wonderful adventure—maybe even a dangerous one.

Supper over, and the after-supper chores finished, and Charlotte Ann had been put to bed by day, and for some new reason had gone to sleep almost right away, Mom and Dad and I sat on the back steps for awhile in the twilight, waiting for night to come.

From the trees across the road, there was the sound of hundreds of locusts whooping it up, and the katydids were doing what katydids do—saying over and over with their raspy voices, "Katy did; Katy, she did; Katy did; Katy, she did—"

There was a breeze fanning our cheeks from across Harm Groenwold's clover field of new mown hay that was as sweet as anything a boy ever smells around Sugar Creek.

Pretty soon, as the afterglow of the sunset faded away, and the orange and red and purplish clouds also faded, a little silver saucer of a moon started shining through the top branches of the walnut tree.

Mom who was used to going to bed as soon as day was over, sighed, looked up at the moon, then said to Dad or to me—or else just said it like she was talking to herself in her mind, and the words came out without her hardly knowing it, "This is my Father's world. There's sleeping splendor in everything."

Dad, who was sitting on the other side of Mom, said, "Yes, but if your husband doesn't get some sleep right now, there won't be any splendor left in him." He yawned then, went out to the iron pitcher pump, pumped a tin cup of water, and brought it back for Mom to drink.

A little stronger breeze came up then, and even in the half dark, from where I sat, I noticed the hollyhocks swaying and their leaves seemed to be whispering something every boy in the world ought to know—and which you already *do* know if you've read the first part of this book.

I was sleepy from having been awake so many hours, but because I was also thirsty, I went out to pump myself a drink, and was surprised to notice how wet the iron handle was.

"Dew doesn't do what Bryant said it did," I managed to think with my sleepy mind. With my voice I yawned back to Dad who was with Mom still sitting on the side porch, "There's dew on the pump handle!"

"On it, or *under* it?" Dad asked back.

Still wide enough awake to remember the two long words he had used on me in the morning, I said, "On the *inferior* as well as the *superior* side." And it felt fine to be able to use such long words and to understand their meaning.

Seven minutes later, more or less, when I was in my upstairs room skinning myself out of my clothes, I looked out the window under the ivy leaves that slanted across the left top corner, and saw the garden in the moonlight, the chicken house, the shadow of old Red Addie's apartment hog house, and off to the right, the apiary where I knew that at least until morning, the bee battle was over.

Then, because a boy's mind can't think very well when he is as tired and yawny-sleepy as I was, I knelt beside the bed for what turned out to be a very short prayer. I can't even remember what most of it was, I was so sleepy. But I do remember that the first part of it was about Circus, who had saved Charlotte Ann like a mother hen gathering one lone chicken under her wings, and I asked God to help Dragonfly to learn to obey his parents better, so he wouldn't have to get clobbered so hard by such a hot-tempered father. "Please, also," I added, "bless Old Man Paddler in California—and if you ever want the gang to go out there to go fishing in the Pacific Ocean for mackerel and bonitos, we'll be willing to go."

I can't even remember finishing the prayer or climbing into bed to lay my head on Mom's nice clean-smelling, fresh pillowcase, on account of the next thing I knew, it was morning—the morning of another day, which would have a wonderful night, which the gang was going to spend away up in the hills in Old Man Paddler's cabin.

Would there be a mystery or a menace or a danger of some kind where we would have to use our muscles as well as our minds, which would make it a whole lot more interesting than just an adventure of the mind?

And would Dad let me take my .22 along just in case we stumbled onto a bear or some other wild animal that once in a while moved into the Sugar Creek territory?

I was out of bed with a bound, ready for work or anything to make the day move faster. No matter what my parents would ask me to do, I would do it with a cheerful whistle.

A look out the window under the ivy showed me a sunlit garden, with dew shining on the black-seeded Simpson lettuce, and along the fence between the house and the orchard, a row of hollyhocks.

Before making a dive for the head of the stairs to go flying down into the wonderful day—and night—I squinted my eyes at the tall flower-loaded hollyhock stalks and sort of whispered to them, "Will you shut up, please, and let me be ambitious of my own accord?"

Down the stairs I went with a bound, like Santa Claus down the chimney in, "Twas the Night Before Christmas." Then I flew through the house and outdoors and across the barnyard to get to the barn in time to help Dad with the chores. As I passed the iron pitcher pump and the garden gate, it seemed I had never felt better in my life. Boy oh boy oh boy oh boy!

I felt so excited in my mind, I was like a saucy little whirlwind spiraling across a pasture full of new mown hay. At the top of my lungs, I yelled for Old Red Addie and all the world to hear, "Boy oh boy, and *double* boy oh boy!"

Dad, who was out in the middle of a bee yard battlefield, heard me and called back, "You all right? You in your right mind?"

"My mind is *always* right!" I shouted with the best sense of humor I'd had in a long time.

All day long it was more or less like that, until it came time for me to get started to meet the gang at the sycamore tree for our hike to Old Man Paddler's cabin. I had been such a cooperative boy, seeing more things to do than I ordinarily saw, and waking up a lot of the sleeping splendor everywhere around the place.

At the grape arbor, I stopped, thinking how much I wanted to take my .22 along. When Dad said "No," it was with a very firm voice. "No, and no, and *double* no!

Making a last desperate effort to show him how important I thought it was, I reminded him, "But you remember we killed a bear and a wildcat and—"

"I *do* remember," he said, "and now that they're both dead and have been for some time, you won't have to worry about them anymore. See?"

Seeing the beech switches on the lower horns of the gun rack just below the .22, I saw a lot more than I saw, and was glad the phone rang right then two long longs and a very short short. The call was for me, and it was Poetry telling me to be sure to remember to bring Old Man Paddler's letter. "I just thought of something important," he told me. "I think maybe *we* are the ones who are supposed to be smart enough to solve the code and find a treasure in a tin box."

Like somebody turned on a light in a dark room, my disappointment at not getting to take my rifle along, was gone, and I was cheerful again.

I quickly ran back upstairs to get the letter, which I'd left on my bed table, where I'd been writing to thank the old man for the seven pictures of George Washington; and when, a little later, I joined the gang at the sycamore tree at the mouth of the cave, that letter was safely in my shirt pocket again.

7

One thing that had made me feel so cheerful all day was the news we got on our party-line phone about ten o'clock in the morning. Circus was feeling fine again, the swelling in his vocal cords was all gone, and he was going to be able to holler and give loon calls like he always does when we're out in the woods together, which goes to show how fast a boy can get well—or almost well—when he keeps his body and mind in good condition. Now the whole gang would be together for our overnight in the old man's cabin.

Poetry was so sure the old man wanted us to solve the code and find a treasure in a tin box that he was bubbling over with excitement. He was also sure of something else, which he asked me to keep a secret.

"It's what I dreamed last night," he

whispered to me, while he and I were alone near the sycamore tree.

I looked all around to be sure nobody else was listening, and this is what he said to me, "You know how in real life the criminal returns to the scene of the crime, and that's where the police or the detectives wait for him—and capture him?"

It was a worrisome idea, especially when my fat, detective-minded friend added, "I dreamed the vandals broke out of custody and they are using the old man's cabin for a hideout."

"Anybody can dream anything!" I answered him.

He scoffed at my doubts. "All right, you wait and see. Here, let me take another look at the code."

He unfolded the letter, turned it over, and squinted his eyes at the ABC's on the back, and then let out a whistle which different ones of the gang heard and came running to see what was going on.

With that, Poetry gave me his secret wink, yawned, and gave the letter a toss in my direction, saying, "Bill answered the letter this morning. Hey, everybody, hadn't we better get going? We want to get the lawn mowed and all the other chores done before dark!"

The path through the swamp, like it always is, was one of the most interesting places in the whole Sugar Creek territory—so many important things having happened there. One of the most important I remembered when we passed a certain narrow place near the muskrat pond. It was the rescue of the Till boys' father, John Till, who, when he was drunk one night, wandered off the path and had sunk all the way down to his chin before we heard him crying for help and rescued him.

"Right out there is where we saved Bob and Tom's father's life!" Dragonfly called out, as we went panting past.

John Till and his two boys were about the only other people who knew the safe way through the swamp—except of course, our fathers.

In about fifteen more minutes—in fact, in only about ten—we were through the swamp and up in the hills and inside the old man's clapboard cabin, where the late afternoon sun was pouring in through the dusty windows, which we decided we would have to wash the next time we came up.

We stood looking around at different things—the cookstove, the firewood in the woodbox, and a bed in a far corner. Above the kitchen table was the prayer map with all the different colored pins in it showing where the old man's missionary friends were, and for whom he prayed every day, whenever he happened to look at the map.

Poetry and I kept stealing secret glances at each other, each of us thinking what if the vandals *had* come back and were using the cabin for a hideout? *If* they were, there'd be some evidence of some kind somewhere.

"Bill," Poetry right then said to me, "want to run upstairs with me to see if the rain's been coming in the windows or anything?"

And that's when I began to get the shivers. At the window that looked out over the old man's backyard and the woodshed, Poetry let out a gasp.

"What!" I whispered to him from behind him.

"The window's unlocked. I'm sure I locked it the last time we were here."

"We'd better lock it again," I said, and started to do it, but he stopped me. "Leave it *un*locked so he can get in tonight while we're asleep."

It was a scary thought—six boys asleep on the floor, somebody climbing into the window upstairs, and sneaking *down*stairs like an Indian looking for white boys' scalps and—

I must have had a worried look on my face, 'cause Poetry said, "All right, kid. I was just fooling. As you said back there at the sycamore tree, 'anybody can dream anything.' I slipped the latch on the window myself when you weren't looking."

Downstairs we went, and outdoors and all of us flew into the work—mowing the lawn, pouring water into the circular, funnel-shaped holes around the newly set-out trees, carrying drinking water from the spring for ourselves and for the birdbaths on the patio, refilling with red-colored, sweetened water, several long slender bottles hanging from the porch ceiling for the humming birds.

I was now trying to give up the idea Poetry had planted in my mind about the vandals returning to the scene of the crime, but it wasn't easy. My mind and I kept looking for clues to prove I was right, or that *he* had been right in the first place.

When Little Jim called us to say the wind had blown down the old man's telephone line and broken it in two, I rushed over to study the ends to see if the line might have been cut with pliers—but it hadn't been. It was easy to see that a tree branch had fallen on it and pulled it loose from where it was fastened to the house.

After quite a while, the chores were all finished; our campfire supper was over; and it was dark, and time for six boys to go to sleep. First, though, we had our garden time. Big Jim had Little Jim read the Twenty-third Psalm; then we had about two minutes of silent prayer, each one thinking his own prayer to God, before Big Jim himself made a prayer out loud for different things—one of the requests being for a boy named Lawrence Bowen, who had the same name as Old Tom the trapper's great-grandnephew.

Pretty soon we were all in our nightclothes and ready for bed. Even though it was night, the moon was still up, so there wasn't anything scary about sleeping alone in a cabin in the hills away from our folks.

For quite a while we lay there in our sleeping bags on the floor and told each other stories, and then because even a boy on an adventure like ours gets sleepy, I drifted off into what somebody once called the land of Nod.

Say! Did you ever all of a sudden in the middle of the night wake out of a sound sleep to imagine a noise of some kind in another room, or a sound at a window like somebody prying *open* a window?

That, all of an eerie sudden, is what happened to me. I jumped awake like I had been shot at, and stared into the black darkness of the cabin, listening with tense nerves and muscles.

And then, as plain as lightning, I saw in another room a light go on and as quickly go off again. I pinched myself to see if I was awake, and I was. The moon must have gone down 'cause it was pitch-dark — or else the sky had clouded over. But what on earth in the middle of the night—and why, and who and how come and—what does a boy do at a cringing time like that!

Now there was a crackling sound, like pine boards burning in a fireplace. Like, also, a key being turned in a rusty lock.

My right arm reached over to touch Poetry awake—and he wasn't there!

I sat up then—*straight* up—and looked around in the black dark to see if the rest of the gang were there, and they were—anyway, there were shadows on the floor all around me like boys under blankets. Also, there was the sound of Dragonfly's crooked nose snoring, which I tried to tell myself in my mind, was the sound I thought I'd heard of a key turning in a rusty lock.

Except for the breathing of the rest of the gang and the sound of pine trees outside soughing in the wind, everything now was as still as the mouse the night before Christmas.

Still, that is, until I heard the crackling sound again in that other room. The light also went on again and this time it stayed on—and then I was startled half out of my wits, on account of I heard Poetry give a surprised whistle.

A second later, I heard his hissing whisper as he said, "Bill! Come here. *Quick!*"

I crawled my trembling self into the other room where he was—and he had the flashlight focused on Old Man Paddler's secret code.

"I've got it!" he whispered. "I've figured out where the tin box with the treasure in it is."

We listened to see if we had wakened the rest of the gang—and we had.

In less time than it takes me to write this, there were six boys in different colored pajamas in a semicircle around that flashlight-lit letter listening to Poetry explain the code.

"It's as simple as ABC," he said. "You take the first letter of the *third* row of letters, which is *h;* look for the *h* in the *second* row, and the letter right above it in the *first* row is *s*. That *s* is the first letter of the word we're after.

"Now," Poetry went on, "take the *second* letter in the third row, which is *z*. Find the *z* in the *second* row, and the letter straight above it in the *first* row is *a*. That *a* is the *second* letter in the word we're after.

"Keep on doing it and you have the answer. I've already done it, and here is the answer:

"Sawdust woodshed! That," Poetry finished with a proud-voiced flourish, "is where we'll find the treasure—in a pile of sawdust in the woodshed!"

It made sense—the kind of sense that made six boys decide to go stealing out into the midnight shadows and move stealthily along the row of newly-set-out trees, following the little circles of light made by our two flashlights.

I don't know why we were keeping so quiet—nor why we decided to creep along in the shadows of the row of evergreens, unless it was that we felt like we were sneaking up on something or somebody. We often did that in make-believe adventures, when we were imagining ourselves to be ambushing an Indian camp or a robbers' hideout.

In a little while we reached the woodshed's only door. Big Jim had his key out and was about to push it into the lock, when he stopped stock-still, his hand poised with the shining key.

"Sh!" he cautioned us. "Lights off!"

Both our flashlights went off, and I tell you it *was* dark.

I didn't need anybody to tell me to shush 'cause whatever it was, I heard it too—a sound of some kind on the other side—on the *inside* of that woodshed door.

Something or somebody—or a ghost *without* a body was in the old man's woodshed.

8

If there had been any time to think or to listen, I might have figured out what kind of a sound it was and who or what was making it. But right then, Big Jim's very brave trembling voice shouted out, *"Who's there? Come on out with your hands up!"*

Now, how in the world could anybody come out with his hands up, when the only door there was, was still locked!

When nobody came out, on account of nobody could anyway, Big Jim unlocked the door, and we all stepped back, he swung the door open and again ordered whoever was inside to come out.

"We're going to count ten!" Big Jim barked, for some reason there being less tremble in his voice than there had been.

"One — two — three — four — five — six — seven — eight — nine — ten!"

But still nobody came out, and there wasn't any sound. We pushed our flashlights in ahead of us and looked in, and the woodshed was as bare as Old Mother Hubbard's cupboard—bare of people, that is. Of course, the old man's garden tools were there, and his workbench with his carpenter's tools such as a saw, a square, chisels, a hammer, and a level, arranged very neatly on the wall above it.

Also above the workbench, was the open window.

"How come the window's open!" Poetry asked. "It was shut the last time we were up here!" I couldn't tell whether he meant it or was only fooling again.

And then all of a flurrying sudden, there was a noise from somewhere up on a wide ledge near the woodshed roof, and a feathery something with spread wings, grayish white with dark specks, went swooping through the air with the greatest of ease, straight through that wide-open window and out into the night.

"Barn owl!" Little Jim cried excitedly and also very happily. "We got one nesting in our barn. D'you see his heart-shaped face and the dark streaks on his tail and wings?"

Well, that was another that! We had all heard something while we were still outside, but now that I knew what had caused it, I remembered it had been the same kind of sound I'd heard barn owls make many a time, a trembling-voiced cry like a screech owl might make if it had a bad cold and somebody was trying to choke it with his hands.

That being settled, we brought our minds back to Old Man Paddler's code. Finding a pile of sawdust in the corner under the workbench, we began to dig—that is, Big Jim did—and in less time than it takes to dig a hill of sweet potatoes in our garden, we had unearthed a small green, tin box about six inches long, one inch deep and three or four inches wide.

In the box, when we opened it was a folded sheet of paper, which when we had *un*folded it, we read—all of us crowding in close, with our heads together. and one flashlight shining on it:

> A bright young boy, as smart as a fox,
> Studied a code and found a tin box;
> And in the tin box, a treasure so rare,
> Nor silver nor gold with its worth could compare.

We quick looked in the bottom of the box for the treasure, and there wasn't a thing—not until we spied a printed note at the side of the piece of paper, which looked like another code. I got as far in my reading of it as "Pr. twenty-two, one—" when there was another sound

119

behind us, like another owl taking wing. I quickly swung my flashlight around to see what it was and it wasn't a *what!*

It was a *who!* Somebody about Big Jim's size, dressed in gray jeans and a T-shirt of some color or other, streaked out from behind a large box under the other end of the workbench and headed for the wide open door!

Well, I'd seen six hounds which had been on a coon trail at night, all of a bawling, barking, full-crying sudden, swing aside from the trail and go bellowing off in another direction after a jumped fox, leaving the coon trail to get cold, while they galloped through the creek bottom, the woods and along the fencerows after the fox.

It must have been something like that, the way we left the poem and the tin box and the treasure that wasn't there, anyway, and took off through the open woodshed door straight for Old Man Paddler's cabin running pell-mell after the boy in the gray jeans and bright colored T-shirt.

Running, panting, dodging brush piles, jumping over a lawn mower, skirting the row of evergreens, splashing up the little brook to the old man's spring, leaping across, and with our

flashlights following him, that boy ran—
straight for the swamp, it looked like.

"I knew I dreamed the truth!" Poetry
puffed behind me. "The criminal returns to his
crime."

Truth or not, I didn't care right then. One
worry that was bigger than my mind, was
putting wings on my feet, and I was flying faster
than a barn owl after a runaway field mouse. I
was remembering that there was only one safe
way through the swamp and that was the one
the gang took. To get off the path on *either*
side was dangerous—but to get off to the
right, on the other side of the pond, would
be to get out into the quicksand!

If the boy we were chasing was one of the
vandals—maybe Lawrence Bowen himself
—then we'd better help answer our own prayers
by saving his life.

A crazy thought came to me right
then—and maybe I ought not even tell you
about it—but it was this: If I had had my .22 I
could have ordered him to stop or I'd shoot!

But then, maybe I'd have been so excited I
would have pulled the trigger, and we'd have
had a dead boy on our hands.

And then, all of a shadowy sudden, there
was somebody else running with us—only not

with us but away up ahead of us. My flashlight spotted a pair of overalls with a boy in them, shoot out from behind a papaw bush at the edge of the swamp, and go streaking after our runaway.

In less that half a minute, it seemed, that faster-running hound of a boy who had just joined our chase had caught up with the woodshed boy, tackled him like Dragonfly had tackled Poetry in the first part of this story, and down they went.

Down also all the rest of us went in a flurry of sixteen legs, sixteen arms, and eight different-pitched voices, calling and talking excitedly and grunting while thousands of muscles held on for dear life to whoever our prisoner was.

Also, we didn't know yet who had joined our chase and outrun us and made the tackle for us—not until Little Jim cried out, *"Big Bob Till!* Where'd you come from!"

And it was Big Bob Till, who used to be the worst enemy the gang ever had. Like a neighbor's hound joining in on a coon chase, he had all of a sudden come in from the shadows and given us the help we needed.

*   *   *

In a little while, all eight of us were inside

the cabin, a kerosene lamp was lit, and we were questioning our prisoner, like police do when they capture somebody. We had tied the boy into a chair so he wouldn't make a break for liberty and make us have to catch him again.

Quite a few things had to be explained. First we found out that Bob Till, who had captured this same boy before, the runaway being one of the vandals, had been listening to a late news program at home, and the announcer had told about one of the vandals that escaped and might be in the Sugar Creek hills.

"I knew the gang was spending the night here," Bob said, "so I decided to come and warn you to be on the lookout."

That's when our prisoner cut in to say, "I didn't break out. I didn't run away. Somebody left the door unlocked, and I just walked out. I had a letter from the old man who lives here, telling me I had the same name as a nephew of somebody called Old Tom the trapper, and I might be old Tom's great grandnephew. He told me that when I got out to come and see him, that he wanted to forgive me for everything, and he had a present for me that used to belong to my uncle—if he *was* my uncle."

And do you know what? I looked across the lamplit space between me and Lawrence

Bowen, if that was his name, and saw him swallow hard, like there was a lump in his throat—and it seemed like I wanted to untie the ropes and set him free.

"You have the letter?" Big Jim asked, and the boy nodded.

"In my right hip pocket," he said.

It was from Old Man Paddler, all right—the same handwriting as that in the letter we had gotten yesterday morning.

Part of it was about Old Tom the trapper, but the part that brought actual tears to my eyes was where Old Man Paddler's trembling old scrawl said, "I'll be leaving California before long, and when you get out, I want you to come to see me. I have a very warm feeling in my heart for you, because of the kind way your dear old uncle Tom used to treat me and my brother so many years ago. I know he would want me to love you and forgive you for his sake, just as the heavenly Father is willing to forgive anyone for Jesus' sake."

There was more to the letter, but none of it that was any of our business, so we tucked it back in Lawrence Bowen's right hip pocket, then we held a meeting to decide what to do.

It was Bob who came up with the right idea

when he said, "You'll have to give yourself up to the police. I know, 'cause once my father—"

Bob's voice choked, and he couldn't say a word on account of his throat had tears in it—and I knew why. Before John Till had been saved from being a drunkard, he'd been in jail quite a few times, and once he had broken out and had to go back and stay another month because of it.

I saw Big Jim, who used to be Bob's worst-hated enemy, reach out a hand and touch Bob's shoulder. And it was just like that hand had a voice and it was saying, "Don't worry. We like you, and we like your dad too."

"Even though the door *was* left open," Big Jim decided for Lawrence Bowen, "you shouldn't have left. Bob's right. You'll have to give yourself up."

Lawrence himself spoke up then. "You think the old man will forgive me for prying open his woodshed window and going in to sleep there? When he wasn't home, I thought maybe he'd be back tomorrow, so I decided to wait. I didn't break into the *cabin!*"

And that explained that. It also reminded Lawrence Bowen of something all of us in our new excitement had forgotten. "What about the tin box—the one you dug out of the sawdust?"

It was like coming back from another world.

Pretty soon, Big Jim had unfolded the note we'd found in the box, and in a jiffy Little Jim came up with the answer to what "Pr. twenty-two, one" meant. "That's the first verse of the twenty-second chapter of Proverbs in the Bible," he said.

At first I thought I was going to be disappointed because there wasn't any actual treasure. But after we had untied Lawrence Bowen, he asked to read the verse out of the Bible for us, and I felt as light as a feather inside. Happier, even, than a boy zigzagging along in the center of a whirlwind or skinning a cat on the crossbeam of a grape-arbor trellis.

Lawrence Bowen surprised me at being able to read so well, and what he read was like a row of Golden Bantam sweet corn rustling in the wind in somebody's garden. Those words out of the old man's big family Bible were,

A good name is rather to be chosen than great riches, and loving favor rather than silver or gold.

When I looked at the shining eyes of our just released prisoner, it seemed I was seeing a lot more than a vandal who could chop a hole in a fishing boat or upset Sarah Paddler's tombstone. I was seeing a boy who, if he had a chance, could grow up to become a man with as good a name as anybody, and that good name would make him richer than the richest person in the world.

Big Bob Till stood up then and said firmly, "I'll have to be going now."

Big Jim answered, getting to his own feet just as Bob reached the cabin door, "Might as well stay all night now that you're here."

"Can't," Bob said back. "Mother would worry—and I promised her."

A few seconds later, he was gone, running as fast as he could in the light of his flashlight. When he passed the old man's spring and swung downhill toward the path that went through the swamp, it seemed like I was seeing not a former enemy but a famous hero, riding a white horse and calling out, "Hiyo Silver!"

Moody Press, a ministry of the Moody Bible Institute, is designed for education, evangelization and edification. If we may assist you in knowing more about Christ and the Christian life, please write us without obligation to: Moody Press, c/o MLM, Chicago, Illinois 60610.